TRAGEDY
GIRL

TRAGEDY GIRL

CHRISTINE HURLEY DERISO

Woodbury, Minnesota

First Edition
First Printing, 2016

Book design by Bob Gaul
Cover design by Lisa Novak
Cover image by iStockphoto.com/61823804/©AJ_Watt

Flux, an imprint of Llewellyn Worldwide Ltd.

Library of Congress Cataloging-in-Publication Data
Names: Deriso, Christine Hurley, 1961– author.
Title: Tragedy girl / Christine Hurley Deriso.
Description: First edition. | Woodbury, Minnesota : Flux, [2016] |
    Summary: "Seventeen-year-old Anne, grieving the death of her parents, thinks she has found a soulmate in her classmate Blake, whose girlfriend has died, until she begins to sense that something about Blake is not what it seems"—Provided by publisher. | Description based on print version record and CIP data provided by publisher; resource not viewed.
Identifiers: LCCN 2016002604 (print) | LCCN 2015045467 (ebook) |
    ISBN 9780738747033 | ISBN 9780738747866 ()
Subjects: | CYAC: Grief—Fiction. | Secrets—Fiction.
Classification: LCC PZ7.D4427 (print) | LCC PZ7.D4427 Tr 2016
    (ebook) | DDC
    [Fic]—dc23
LC record available at http://lccn.loc.gov/2016002604

Flux
Llewellyn Worldwide Ltd.
2143 Wooddale Drive
Woodbury, MN 55125-2989
www.fluxnow.com

To my sweetie, the best of the good guys.
I love you, Graham.

ONE

"Knock 'em dead, E. May I suggest the leopard-print leggings?"

I squint to read the text as blanched sunlight seeps through the blinds of my new bedroom.

"No, you may not," I murmur sleepily to myself with a smile. Leave it to Sawyer, my best friend from back home, to make sure I start even the least promising day with a smile.

I lean up on an elbow and glance at the clock on my bedside table: 6:20 a.m. The first day of my senior year will start in approximately ninety minutes. Whoop.

Sawyer never lets me forget the time I was sent home from school in tenth grade for a dress-code violation, prompting my impassioned Zola-esque speech about leggings fitting every criterion of pants, particularly when paired with a shirt that practically hit my knees. Sawyer rewarded me with a slow clap, but I still got sent home. "Leopard-print leggings" have been our most well-worn meme ever since.

"*Muah, Sawbones*," I text back, then sign off with my customary "*E.*" He's called me that since I emphasized when we met in grade school that my name was *Anne with an E*. He actually called me that for a long time—*Anne with an E*—then switched it up for a while by calling me *E with an Ann*—then shortened it permanently to E. My parents' joint funeral three months ago was the only time he ever called me just "Anne," a formality that chillingly drove home the new identity foisted on someone associated with a Terrible Tragedy.

That "Anne" seared my soul, made me realize I'd never be free of pity smiles or strained formality in my hometown ever again, even from Sawyer. It took a while to work out the details, but I decided then and there to accept my aunt and uncle's offer and move three hundred and forty miles away to their home in the beach town of Hollis, South Carolina—on tiny Hollis Island—for my last year of high school.

So here I am.

Yet what have I really gained? Now, I get pity smiles and strained formality from my aunt and uncle rather than my friends back home. Not that I don't appreciate their kindness. They're just too earnest when they stress, for instance, that I should call this room *my* room rather than their spare bedroom, or that I should help myself to whatever I want in the kitchen because, hey, it's my kitchen too! I miss the day when things just *were*. Let's face it: when someone has to point out that a kitchen is your kitchen too, it's not really your kitchen.

I put the phone down, swallow hard, and head to the bathroom (*my* bathroom, Aunt Meg perkily insists) for one of my three-minute showers.

Short showers and lightning-fast styling time are why I chopped off my auburn hair after Mom and Dad's accident. I can't stand the deafening hum of a blow dryer anymore. Who can afford to be lulled by the sound of white noise when god-knows-what can be unfolding just down the street? After all, I'd been in the shower that evening, deliciously oblivious as I massaged cucumber and sage-scented shampoo into my waist-length hair, when a drunk driver ran a stop sign and crashed into my parents' car.

I'm not superstitious; I know awful things can happen whether or not I happen to be in the shower, or whether or not I'm being lulled into complacency by the white noise of a blow dryer. Still... vigilance. That's my new approach to life. Then, even if the unthinkable happens, at least I'll be paying attention.

I don't know much anymore, but I know that I'll never, ever let myself be blindsided again.

———

"Your first day!"

I smile weakly. Aunt Meg starts lots of conversations like this—blurting out a basic, obvious fact—but I know she means well.

"Yep," I say, standing at the kitchen counter pouring milk over my cereal.

She tightens the sash around her pale-pink bathrobe, walks closer, and fingers my hair, still damp from the shower.

"Your haircut's so cute," she says. "So sporty and spunky,

but still really elegant. Your cheekbones look amazing with short hair."

"Thanks, Aunt Meg."

She flicks a lock of blonde hair over her shoulder.

"Maybe we can get pedicures this weekend," she suggests, and I nod, biting my lower lip as I glance through the kitchen window at the pine trees swaying in the back yard. I feel so claustrophobic in this house sometimes. I imagine myself running at full speed into the woods, my arms pumping as my sneakers plow down the twigs and bracken in my path.

"Of course, you'll have friends to get pedicures with soon," Aunt Meg says, seeming to intuit my lack of enthusiasm. Damn. I try hard not to tip my hand; she's been so great to me, you know?

Aunt Meg sips coffee from her mug, then adds, "I know you'll make friends in no time."

I nod noncommittally.

"And boyfriends! We'll be shopping together soon for prom dresses!"

I pinch my lips together. "Aunt Meg, I'm mostly just going to concentrate on my schoolwork this year. You know ... try to keep my grades up so I can get a scholarship ... "

"Of course, of course. But there's always time for fun."

She rests a cool palm on my cheek and I will my eyes not to fill with tears.

"Sure," I say softly. "I'm sure I can squeeze in some fun. Aunt Meg, my cereal's getting soggy ... "

"Oh, of course, of course. Go eat, sweetie," Aunt Meg says, sweeping her arm toward the kitchen table.

I give her an apologetic look—I find myself giving her apologetic looks approximately forty times a day—and walk to the table. As I settle into my seat, Uncle Mark walks in, his dark hair tousled as he straightens a tie. He looks so much like my dad.

"'Morning, sunshine," he says, and I'm not sure who he's talking to. I raise a hand awkwardly in response. He pecks Aunt Meg on the lips, then sits next to me at the table.

"Gorgeous day outside," he says, and I *mmmmm* my agreement. "It's supposed to be nice all week. Maybe we can go to the beach this weekend."

Oh god. Are my aunt and uncle going to be tripping over each other for the rest of the year to try to fill my weekends with fun and otherwise overcompensate for my having two dead parents? I'm not sure how much faux cheer I can muster from one offer to the next.

I yearn for the days when Uncle Mark and Aunt Meg were merely bit players in my life, perfectly nice people with cameo roles offering infusions of warm hugs and affable questions about how I was doing in school. They are no longer just the people who spend random weekends with me and bring me presents on special occasions. Now, their personalities, their quirks, their idiosyncrasies are the wallpaper of my daily existence. Even calling them Aunt and Uncle—I'd always dispensed with that formality before. They were just Mark and Meg. But now, being casual seems so ... ungrateful. I feel dizzy as I contemplate the new normal of squelching annoyances and showing gratitude on a day-to-day, hour-to-hour, minute-to-minute basis.

Still, a day at the beach doesn't sound half bad. At least, it *wouldn't* have sounded half bad … in my old world. I can't help but feel nostalgic as I contemplate a carefree day wiggling my toes in the sand. I remember what a treat it used to be to visit Uncle Mark and Aunt Meg when I was younger— my beach relatives! My parents and I would sit right at this table eating fresh grapefruit for breakfast, then grab our beach towels and zoom out the door for the ten-minute drive to the shore. I'd surf with Dad and Uncle Mark, then shake the water from my ears as I joined Mom and Aunt Meg for a stroll on the beach. We'd read cheesy novels, snack on chips, push our beach chairs back from the tide periodically, and basically loll away the day, splashing in the surf at regular intervals.

At the end of a long day, our cheeks rosy, we'd head back to the house—this house—for boiled shrimp and water-melon slices on the redwood deck, licking our fingers and laughing as Felix the Lab chased one tennis ball after another. Then we'd come to the sunroom and collapse on the cozy overstuffed furniture with ceiling fans whirring overhead, crickets chirping in the backyard pines.

This house was a retreat back then, an oasis. Aunt Meg's exuberance was a sunny punctuation mark on our lazy beach days—a stark contrast to my droll, witty mom—and Uncle Mark's resemblance to my dad was nothing more than a fleeting, offhand observation, as opposed to a jolting stab of pain.

Nothing about them, nothing about this house, feels the same any more. I wasn't meant to *live* in this beauti-ful sunny home; I wasn't meant to smile politely on a daily basis during well-meaning conversations about pedicures and prom dresses, particularly at 6:45 in the morning. I love Aunt Meg and Uncle Mark, but I want my house back. I want my wordless grumpy mornings back. I want my parents back. I want my life back.

"Nervous about today?" Uncle Mark asks.

I shake my head, averting my eyes from his hopeful gaze.

"Nah," I say, aiming for breezy. "Hey, I'm going to school with a bunch of beach bums. How challenging can it be?"

He raises an eyebrow approvingly. "Cocky and over-confident, huh? I like it."

"That's me, alright."

He glances at my cereal bowl and says, "Wheaties again? That was always your dad's favorite, you know."

I raise my spoon gamely. "The breakfast of champions."

Lots of this goes on at my new home, too: references to my parents—comparisons, reminiscences, offhand comments. The references come so fast and seem so forced, I can't help but get the feeling my aunt and uncle consulted with a therapist who recommended this strategy. I'm touched by the gesture, and sure, it helps to weave my parents into the conversation, but nothing seems natural anymore. I wonder what it would be like to have a conversation that doesn't seem guided by the invisible hand of a professional.

Uncle Mark smiles at me as I take a bite, then leans into his elbows and says softly, "You know we've got your back ... right?"

I lock eyes with him for a long moment. "Yes," I say, and

return Aunt Meg's smile as she looks over her shoulder at me from the kitchen sink. "I know you do."

"Good," Uncle Mark tells me, rising from his chair and kissing my cheek. "Don't ever forget that."

TWO

"Forget it."

I shut my locker door and turn toward the sound of a voice inexplicably addressing me.

"Excuse me?" I say.

The girl swirls her index finger through a lock of long dark hair and flashes a conciliatory smile. "Oh, I didn't mean anything by it. Just ... I mean, I heard you're new, and I thought you'd want a heads-up that he's definitely unavailable."

Truly, I have no clue what she's talking about.

"Blake," she clarifies.

My mind zips through its database for context but comes up dry. What the hell is she talking about?

"You were just checking out Blake Fields," she says.

Aaaaaahhh. I still have no idea what she's talking about, but I'm catching on that cattiness is alive and well at Hollis Island

9

High School. I'm tempted to peer cryptically at this presumptuous twit, as if trying to glean the depths of her audacity—that definitely would have been my MO back home in Dixonville—but even though my first day at Hollis Island High is almost over, I'm still dutifully in new-girl mode.

I flick my bangs from my eyes. "Blake Fields...?" I venture, in as unthreatening a tone as I can manage.

She points at the locker next to mine. "The guy you were just checking out," she says, sounding a little irked at my obtuseness.

And really, what's the point in trying to convince her that the only thing I was checking out was my calculus book. "Right," I say instead. "Unavailable. Got it. Thanks for the tip."

A look of exasperation clouds her face. "I *mean* it," she insists petulantly. "Didn't you hear what happened?"

"Didn't get the memo."

I toss a wave and walk away. So much for my new-girl congeniality. I'm still clueless about what this twit is insinuating, but however much she's enjoying trying to bait me, I have got to cut her playtime short.

A girl I've seen in my morning classes approaches me with a subtle smile and a single raised eyebrow. "Getting to know Natalie?" she asks.

"I'm apparently not supposed to notice some guy I've never noticed," I say as we walk down the hall. "She put me on notice."

The girl laughs. "Headed for Calculus?" she asks me.

I nod.

"Me too. I'm Melanie."

"Hi. I'm Anne. I think I've seen you in a couple of my classes?"

Melanie nods. "So, who aren't you supposed to notice?"

"Um ... sorry, I've forgotten his name."

"Clearly, you're obsessed," Melanie says, and we laugh lightly, moving with the flow of traffic down the hall.

"Good thing what's-her-name nipped that in the bud," I say dryly.

Melanie nods her head to signal me to take a left, and we flow into the math wing of the school. "Natalie's insecurities go into overdrive when she sees somebody new," Melanie says. "She's like, *Whoa, new-girl alert! Better teach her the pecking order really fast so she doesn't go around thinking she owns the place.*"

"So I don't own Hollis Island High? Bummer."

Melanie snaps a finger. "Oh, I bet I know who she was talking about. Blake Fields?"

"Yeah, I think."

"Oh, don't *even*," Melanie teases as I follow her into our Calculus class, lightly brushing shoulders with people leaving. "He's not only gorgeous, he's tragic. Now, *that's* some serious cachet."

I follow her to the far end of the room, Melanie giving fluttery waves to classmates as she passes them. I settle into the seat beside her.

"What's tragic about him?" I ask as we put our books on our desktops.

"His girlfriend died over the summer," Melanie says, then glances at me for a sensitivity check. "Which, of course, really is sad."

"How did she die?"

Melanie pushes a lock of dark blonde hair behind her ear. "Drowned. In the ocean."

I mouth *Wow.* "Did you know her?"

Melanie shakes her head. "She went to Cloverville High—the school in the next town over. Plus, she was younger than us... she'd be a junior this year, I think."

The sixth-period bell rings and a teacher in shirt sleeves and a bow tie tells us to settle down.

"Mr. Loring," Melanie whispers conspiratorially. "We call him Mr. Boring."

"Aaaahh. Clever."

"Before we get started," Mr. B/Loring begins in a monotone, "we'd like to welcome a new student to our class. Uh, Annie...?"

"It's Anne," I say softly. "Anne Welch."

He responds with an awkwardly prolonged pity smile. Damn. He's at least the fourth teacher today to give me a pity smile. Not even three hundred and fifty miles is far away enough to escape them.

"Well." He tilts his head, his eyes oozing sympathy. "Welcome, Anne."

"Well. Thanks."

The class chuckles lightly. Uh-oh. Was that a smartass response? The last thing I want to do is draw attention to myself. Hollis Island High is just a brief way station en route to college. Now, that'll be a *true* fresh start. This is a year I'm simply trying to endure.

"I certainly hope you'll find this class enjoyable," he says improbably, because truly, what are the odds.

But I just smile and nod.

Low profile, E, I remind myself, fingering the wedding rings that dangle under my shirt from a chain around my neck, my only 24-7 connection to my parents. *Low profile.*

———————

"So!"

Another oh-so-nuanced conversation starter from Aunt Meg. She spoons some mashed potatoes onto her plate and passes me the bowl.

"How was your first day of school?" she asks.

"Okay," I respond, spooning my portion and passing the bowl along to Uncle Mark. "I take it the word's out to all my teachers about Mom and Dad?"

Aunt Meg feigns confusion. "What do you—"

"We talked to the counselor," Uncle Mark says quietly. "We had to explain your circumstances ... us being your guardians, why you've switched schools your senior year ... "

"Plus, honey, we wanted to make sure they were aware of your special needs," Aunt Meg says, her eyebrows an inverted V.

I stiffen. "Special needs?"

"Just ... that you've been through a lot, and that the administration should be attuned to any ..."

"We know you're fine, Annie," says Uncle Mark, who calls me that sometimes on purpose and not because he's mispronouncing my name. "We just needed to give a little information about your background. I'm sure the curiosity factor will die down in the next couple of days."

"Oh, you know what?" Aunt Meg says in her sing-song voice. "I found a list of extracurriculars on the school website. Plus, volunteer opportunities!"

My fork lands with a dull thud into my mashed potatoes. "Thanks, Aunt Meg, but I don't know if I want to get involved in—"

"Staying busy is key," she says, a stern edge creeping into her perky tone.

"Meg, Annie needs to take things at her own pace." Uncle Mark's voice is kind but firm.

"Busy!" she repeats, her pitch higher than ever. "That's the key! Plus, she's got her college applications to think about." She flashes me a quick smile.

I bite my lip, my heart sinking with the reminder that I'll go the whole year—maybe longer—without being able to have a genuine or spontaneous conversation with the people my school knows as my "guardians."

"Oops. Forgot the rolls," Aunt Meg says, then pushes her chair away from the table and scurries into the kitchen.

Uncle Mark clears his throat, and when I glance at him, he winks at me.

"She'll calm down soon, I promise," he says.

I wave a hand through the air. "Aunt Meg is great," I say, furrowing my brow for emphasis.

"I know she tries too hard," Uncle Mark responds, "especially when she's stressed. But she means well."

My heart sinks. "I'm so sorry I brought stress into your life."

Uncle Mark leans closer. "Honey, no. *No.* That's not what I meant. She's just in hyper-management mode right now, what with getting you enrolled in school and everything. She wants the best for you; we both do. It's just... like I said... she tries a little too hard."

He squeezes my hand as Aunt Meg walks back into the dining room with a bowl full of hot rolls. "Might want to wait a couple of minutes for them to cool down," she says, rejoining us at the table.

I smile weakly and pick at my food. Of *course* I've brought stress into their lives, like it wasn't stressful enough for Uncle Mark to lose his brother and sister-in-law. He and Aunt Meg have been happily childless throughout their twenty-something-year marriage, touring Europe, going on cruises, joining tennis leagues, or redecorating their house whenever they felt like it. Now, they're arranging discreet meetings with high school counselors, enumerating my "special needs," and ensuring that all my credits have transferred. I feel a thud in my stomach as I contemplate that moving here was perhaps the stupidest, most selfish decision I've ever made. I barely know a soul on this island, and though my crash course with grief has made it easy to replace my once-active lifestyle with hours on end of burrowing my nose in a book, I can't deny that my first day of school left me achingly lonely.

"Honey, speaking of your special needs . . ." Aunt Meg says, willfully avoiding Uncle Mark's disapproving scowl. "I think . . . I think it might be a good idea for you to see a therapist."

Ah. The talk-about-her-parents-constantly therapist?

Uncle Mark's eyes are shooting daggers at her, but Aunt Meg is still ignoring him. "I've called around for some references, and this psychologist named Virginia Sennett comes highly recommended. She specializes in working with young—"

"Meg, you should have discussed this with me," Uncle Mark says in a clipped tone, and I wonder if I'll soon be able to add divorce to the ways I've transformed their lives.

Aunt Meg bristles and tells him under her breath, "You know very well we talked about—"

"You know what?" I blurt. "I think that sounds like a good idea."

Their eyes widen.

"I think it'll help, and I really appreciate all the trouble you've gone to," I say.

Long pause.

"You're sure?" Uncle Mark asks, and I nod briskly.

Yes, I'll see a therapist. Anything to dissipate the tension in the room. Anything to loosen the knot in my stomach. Anything to make Aunt Meg smile, and yes, she's smiling now. Anything to assuage my guilt, to be less of a burden, to hasten this journey through Hollis Island hell.

Anything to help me choke down this meat loaf so I can excuse myself from the table at the earliest possible opportunity.

I put a bite in my mouth and swallow it whole.

THREE

"Sorry."

I glance at the guy with dark hair and deep blue eyes who has just accidentally knocked my shoulder with his locker door. I smile. "No problem."

"The door always sticks," he says, explaining why he opened it harder than he intended to.

"Yeah, I'm guessing these lockers date back to, I dunno... maybe the sixth century?"

He smiles. "Nah, you're off by a few million years. We're talking caveman technology here."

I wrinkle my nose. "I think you just insulted cavemen."

We rifle around in our lockers for a moment, then he says, "I'm Blake."

I nod. "Anne."

He extends a hand just as I'm grabbing my first-period

English Lit book from my locker, and I fumble, tucking it hastily under my arm so I can shake.

"Hi," I say.

Blake takes my hand, laughing lightly at my awkwardness.

"Not so good at multitasking," I tell him sheepishly.

A guy with fine, shoulder-length blond hair rushes up to Blake and stops just short of chest-butting him, forcing me to jump back.

"Dude," Blake mutters irritably.

"My notes," the other guy snaps. "I need my notes."

"Fine." Blake opens a notebook, grabs two sheets of paper, and hands it to the guy, who snatches it—*snap!*—from his fingertips and rushes down the hall.

"Already borrowing notes on the second day of school?" I ask with a raised eyebrow as I close my locker door.

But instead of getting the wise-guy response I expect, Blake's eyes fall. "I had kind of a meltdown in Spanish class yesterday and had to go to the nurse's office. I promise, I usually take my own notes."

I push my book tighter against my chest as people rustle past us on their way to their first-period classes. "What was wrong?" I ask. Then the lightbulb goes off over my head. This is the guy Melanie was telling me about yesterday…the guy whose girlfriend died over the summer.

"Just…kind of a panic attack," he explains, still averting his eyes. "It wasn't as dramatic as it sounds; I just felt really claustrophobic all of a sudden and needed some air. I was okay after lying down a few minutes."

I nod. "I know the feeling. Your friend didn't seem very sympathetic."

Blake's eyebrows knit together. "Oh, you mean Jamie? Nah, he didn't mean anything by that."

"Well. Nice to meet you."

He nods, his eyes still doleful.

I take a few steps down the hall, then suddenly pivot and face him again. "Hey, Blake?"

He glances up.

"Feel better ... okay?"

He gives me a thumbs-up sign as his deep-set eyes turn warm.

Warm ... but so incredibly sad.

"So, that guy you were mentioning yesterday—how did you say his girlfriend died?"

Melanie forks a piece of lettuce and pops it in her mouth. "Drowned. In the ocean."

Her friend, Lauren, leans closer into our lunch table. "You know Blake?" she asks me.

I shake my head. "Not really. I met him at my locker this morning, and Melanie mentioned yesterday that his girlfriend died over the summer."

"Natalie informed Anne yesterday that Blake is off limits," Melanie tells Lauren conspiratorially, and they share a knowing smile.

"Natalie's like a narc," Lauren says to me. "Only instead of sniffing out druggies, she sniffs out hot new girls so she can put them on notice: no sucking up her oxygen! She's got dibs on all the studs, even though none of them give her the time of day."

The girls study my reaction, then grin. "You're blushing!" Melanie tells me, and I squeeze my eyes shut and shake my head.

"Sorry; you're the hot new girl whether you like it or not," Lauren says. "The word is out. I've even heard some numbers bandied about. I think the consensus is you're a solid eleven. And this is on a ten-point scale, mind you."

I cringe. "Please."

"You truly can't handle attention," Melanie says.

"Change of subject?" I plead, and the girls laugh good-naturedly at my mortification. Why, oh why, did I bring up Blake in the first place? That's what started all this, which probably made me look like some kind of boy-crazy twit. I just can't get his sad eyes off my mind...

"Okay, new subject," Melanie says. "Why did you move here? Somebody's job? What do your parents do?"

I smile wanly. "Not much. They're dead."

The girls gasp.

"Dead?" Lauren says. "Both of them?"

I nod. "They died in a car crash last spring. I moved here to live with my aunt and uncle."

"Oh *god*," Melanie says. "How do you...what do you...?"

I'm used to this kind of shocked-speechless response, but I know what she means: How do you go on without your parents? What steps are involved in moving on with your life when your foundation has been ripped from underneath you? I offer the answer I've learned from experience: "You remind yourself to breathe," I say.

And I mean it. When I have absolutely no idea how to go on, I talk myself through the process of inhaling, then exhaling. Somehow, one breath leads to another, and another, then another ... *Inhale, exhale, repeat.* If Melanie is looking for any cosmic wisdom or helpful platitudes, she won't learn them from me. I don't know how to make sense from nonsense, or order from chaos, or happiness from misery. I haven't learned any of those lessons yet, and I kind of doubt I ever will. I've just learned to remind myself to breathe.

"I'm so sorry ... " Lauren says in barely a whisper.

"Thanks. But I'm okay. Truly."

An awkward moment hangs in the air, and then Melanie says, "No wonder you and Blake connected."

Connected? Did my offhand comment earlier insinuate that we connected? *Did* we connect? I feel excruciatingly transparent.

"Hey, he's a really nice guy," Melanie adds, seeming to intuit my self-consciousness. "In fact, I heard he was going to the bonfire Friday night, that he's finally ready to start getting out again. We should go. I've got a semi-major crush on his best friend. Speaking of whom ... "

Our eyes follow Melanie's as Blake walks into the cafeteria with the guy who demanded his notes back when I met him at our lockers.

"That's his best friend?" I ask.

"Mmmmmm," Melanie replies, her eyes still on the two of them. "Jamie Stuart."

"He didn't seem very friendly this morning," I say.

Melanie glances at me. "What do you mean?"

I shrug. "Blake had to leave his Spanish class yesterday to go to the nurse's office, and Jamie seemed upset about having to lend him his notes. I mean, I just saw them together for a second, but ... "

"Uh-uh," Melanie insists, shaking her head briskly. "You definitely misinterpreted. Jamie worships the ground Blake walks on."

Lauren nods, her dark hair bouncing lightly on her shoulders. "Blake is like a big brother to him, ultra-protective. Jamie was short and scrawny until last year. Always in Blake's shadow."

"Then he ... blossomed," Melanie says, staring at Jamie as he and Blake collect their trays.

Lauren gives them another once-over and nods. "Yeah. Who would have guessed they'd *both* turn out to be tens?" She gives me a mischievous glance. "Not that they're *elevens*, like you. I mean, how many people can manage that?"

I toss my head backward and groan. "Enough, enough!"

"Definitely plan on the bonfire Friday night," Melanie tells us. "I just might need to borrow Jamie's Spanish notes myself."

"You have *got* to be kidding."

I glance up from the conveyor belt where I've just placed my cafeteria tray and see Natalie facing me, one hand on her hip and a sheet of sleek dark hair falling down her back.

"I beg your pardon?"

"A bonfire? You honestly think Blake would go to a bonfire?"

My brow furrows. Why in the world does this girl keep pulling me into conversations that seem to start in the middle?

"I couldn't help overhearing," she finally clarifies. "Do you and your 'girlfriends' honestly think Blake and Jamie would be caught dead at a bonfire?"

"My 'girlfriends' and I?" I ask, borrowing her air quotes.

"Don't you know that a bonfire is where it happened?"

"*It?*"

Natalie huffs. "The drowning I was trying to tell you about yesterday. If you hadn't rushed off, you would have *heard*. Blake and his friends were at a bonfire on the beach when his girlfriend drowned. To *death.*"

"Oh." I'm annoyed enough to want to walk away but intrigued enough to stay put. Natalie seems to sense my conflict, so she picks up the pace.

"They were having a bonfire on the beach, and Blake's girlfriend decided to take a quick swim. When Blake and Jamie realized she wasn't coming back, they rushed out on Jamie's jet ski to try to find her, but they never did." She pauses for dramatic effect. "Her body was never found."

"Wow," I say softly. "That's terrible. Did she not know how to swim?"

"She could swim, but the surf was really rough that night. We think she got caught in a rip current."

I peer at Natalie closer. "So you were there?"

She rolls her eyes impatiently. "No. But I know practically everybody who was. And, I mean, I was *invited*, of course. I just had other plans. Thank heaven I *didn't* go. Everybody who was there will be traumatized for life." She shakes her head slowly. "As if Blake hadn't already been through enough..."

Okay, I'll bite: "What else has he been through?"

She feigns looking startled by my ignorance. "Uh, duh, *cancer*," she says. "Oh, that's right...you're new. But everybody around here knows Blake had cancer in middle school. It was awful; he just barely survived. We spent a whole year taking turns making him cards and bringing him cookies—his friends did, I mean. His *good* friends. Anyway...cancer...then his girlfriend drowns at a bonfire on the beach..."

She studies me evenly before cutting to the chase: "So I don't think you'll find Blake at a *bonfire* any time soon."

I briefly consider defending myself—who said I was going to a bonfire in the first place?—but I just nod instead. "Got it," I say. "Well, I've got to get to my class. Later."

Natalie's jaw drops slightly, but I'm already on the move.

I feel her eyes bore into my back as I walk away.

FOUR

I close my bedroom door, bite an apple, and settle in at my computer. I've got homework, but first, I do a quick Google search. I don't know the dead girl's name, but I have enough information to find what I'm looking for in just a few seconds:

Officials Halt Search for Possible Drowning Victim

—By Ted Hardiford, *Hollis Island Tribune* Reporter—

Rescuers called off an eleven-hour search Sunday morning for a sixteen-year-old believed to have drowned off Hollis Island.

I interrupt my reading as my eyes drift to the high school yearbook photo of the girl that accompanies the article. Wow... she looks kinda like me, especially now that my hair's short. A *lot* like me, actually ... same almond-shaped eyes, same high cheekbones ... It's kind of eerie. I squeeze my arms across my chest and resume reading:

Cara Costwell, a rising junior at Cloverville High School, was reportedly swimming in the ocean on the north side of the island late Saturday night, June 14, when friends noticed she hadn't returned to their bonfire on the beach as promptly as they expected. Blake Fields and Jamie Stuart, rising seniors at Hollis Island High School and friends of the victim, boarded Stuart's nearby jet ski to look for her. After a fruitless fifteen-minute search, they returned to the beach and called the authorities.

Local police contacted the Coast Guard at 1:15 a.m., reporting Costwell as missing and possibly carried out to sea by unusually strong rip currents. Responders searched throughout the night and Sunday morning.

At noon Sunday, the rescue mission turned into a search for Costwell's remains, which have yet to be recovered.

"It's just devastating suspending a search when someone is still missing, particularly a teenager," said Capt. Harold Roland, commanding officer of ...

"Anne?"

I minimize the screen as Aunt Meg creaks my bedroom door open while knocking on it. I'd love to suggest that the knock precede the creak from now on, but hey, it's her house.

"Hi, Aunt Meg," I say, pushing my chair away from the desk.

"How was your second day of school?" she asks.

"Good," I say, managing a smile. "A couple of girls invited me to join them at lunch, which was really nice of them."

"Great!" Aunt Meg says, her face brightening. "What are their names?"

"Um ... Melanie and Lauren. I have some classes with them. They're really nice."

Aunt Meg's beaming face seems to prod me to add more adjectives, superlatives exuberant enough to match her expression, but I'm already surpassing my perky quota.

"Well, *good for you*," she says, punching every word. "And, honey, you meant what you said last night at dinner about being willing to talk to a therapist? You don't mind having just a few sessions to discuss your ... to talk about whatever?"

I clench my fists but nod. "Yeah, Aunt Meg, it's fine. Whatever you need me to do."

"It's what *you* need," she assures me, walking over and stroking my hair. "Anyway, you've got an appointment next Monday at four p.m. Work for you?"

I swallow hard. "Yep. That's fine."

"Good." She holds my gaze just long enough to make me excruciatingly uncomfortable, then winks and walks out, closing the door behind her.

Okay. Time to bang out my homework. But first ...

I return to the Google search and click on another article:

Memorial Service Lauds "World's Sweetest Girl"

—By Ted Hardiford, *Hollis Island Tribune* Reporter—

High humidity and soaring temperatures made June 28 one of the hottest days so far this summer, but mourners at Cara Costwell's memorial service huddled together midday at Peachtree Park as if they couldn't shake the chill from their bones.

Some literally shivered; others simply wept. But their collective body language spoke volumes: she can't really be gone.

Yet the three-hundred-plus attendees followed Cara's parents' lead in facing the reality of her demise, her unrecovered body notwithstanding.

"We've clung to hope as long as we could," her mother said in a quavering voice as she welcomed the throngs to the service. "But it's time to say goodbye to our little girl. She loved the sea, and now she's there for eternity."

Several of Cara's friends spoke at the service as well, including classmate Rebecca Jowers, who called her the "world's sweetest girl." Hollis Island High School seniors Blake Fields and Jamie Stuart, the two who searched in vain for Cara on a jet ski after realizing she was in peril, were scheduled to speak but sobbed quietly at their seats instead, too shaken to go to the podium.

"I know some of you struggle with guilt," Cara's father said, looking directly at the two young men, "but Cara wouldn't want that, and neither do her mother

and I. You were wonderful friends to Cara, and you did
everything you could to help her that night. The best
way to honor her memory is to move on with your . . . "

My cell phone rings, and I smile when I see the call is
from Sawyer.

"Hey, Sawbones," I say, x-ing out the computer screen.

"'Sup, E. I miss you like mad."

I smile, walk over to my bed, and snuggle against the pil-
lows. "Miss you more. Hey, have you gotten up the nerve to
ask Paul out yet?"

Sawyer snorts. "Yeah. Then I climbed Mount Everest and
cured cancer. Just crossing off the ol' bucket list, one item
after the other."

"*Ask him out*," I scold. "Seeing as you're officially friend-
less since I left town, it's time you broadened your horizons."

We laugh some more, then I nibble a fingernail. "So there's
a guy at my school . . . " I say slowly.

Sawyer sucks in his breath. "Oh god. You're mentioning a
guy on the second day of school?"

"It's nothing," I insist, squeezing my eyes shut and wondering why in the world I brought this up. "I barely even know
him. His locker is next to mine, and we chatted a few minutes
this morning, and . . . "

" . . . and you're in love?"

I roll my eyes and *tsk* at Sawyer. "He's just really . . . sad. He
had cancer when he was younger, and his girlfriend died over
the summer . . . "

"Wow. You squeeze in a lot of chit-chat at your locker."

"No, no," I say, waving a hand through the air. "I just learned a few things about him from other people. But really, isn't that sad?"

"Mmmmm. How did his girlfriend die?"

"*Drowned*," I reply in an appropriately reverent tone. "And he was there. He tried to save her, but he couldn't."

Sawyer pauses, then says, "Hey, E?"

"Yeah."

"I'm thinking you need to take things kinda slow. You've been through a lot lately."

Okay, *that* was annoying.

"I was just mentioning an interesting person I happened to meet," I say in a tight voice.

"C'mon, E, don't get pissed," he cajoles. "And don't pretend there's not some vibe going with this guy. This is me you're talking to. If you just happen to drop one into a conversation on the second day of school, then—"

"Oh my gosh! Wouldn't you consider it a little conversation-worthy if you met somebody whose girlfriend just died tragically?"

Sawyer is silent for a moment, then says, "Don't try to be somebody's savior right now, E. You need some time to get steady on your feet again."

I thrum my fingers against my bedspread. "You know what's weird? My Aunt Meg wants me to see some therapist. If only she knew that you were already covering that base."

Sawyer laughs gamely. "Go ahead and project all your frustrations onto me," he says. "I can take it." But then his voice is somber again:

"Just be careful."

FIVE

"Not *again*."

I laugh lightly. "This is starting to seem personal."

Blake has accidentally bonked my shoulder with his locker door every day this week, and now that it's Friday, the joke has become shorthand.

"Time to take out a restraining order?" I ask.

"Time to sue the locker manufacturer," he replies.

"It would be nice to get through one day of school without bodily injury."

Blake steps in front of me. "Tell ya what: slug me back. Come on, I can take it."

I simulate punching him, and he reels comically.

"Okay," he says, his dark blue eyes sparkling. "We're even now."

"We're even when I say we're even," I say, feigning another punch.

He winces, then leans in closer. "I've got an idea," he says, his voice low. "Let me make it up to you."

I study his dark blue eyes, stalling for time. Am I reading him right? Yes, this would clearly qualify as flirting from any other guy, a guy whose girlfriend hadn't died just a few months earlier. I'm not sure what to think.

"How?" I ask tentatively.

He offers a hint of a smile. "The school's having some lame kickoff party for football season tonight," he says. "Come with me?"

Oh. I guess I *was* reading him right.

"Um ... " I say, still stalling as I press the wedding rings under my shirt against my chest. "I think I kinda made plans to go with my friends ... "

Friends. Do Melanie and Lauren count as friends yet? Does Blake's invitation count as a date? I lived in the same house my whole life before my parents died; I never had to wonder where I stood about *anything*. Now, suddenly, everything seems vague, ambiguous, rife with the potential for embarrassing misinterpretations.

"Melanie and Lauren?" Blake asks, and I nod. I guess he's seen us sitting together at the lunch table all week.

"So maybe we can all go together?" he ventures, cocking his head a bit to the side, a gesture that somehow disarms me by making him look little-boyish. Little-boyish in a tall, incredibly cute kind of way.

"My friend Jamie is coming too, and maybe my brother," he continues. "So, you know, we could go as a group ... ?"

"Um ... "

"Just a suggestion," Blake says, moving subtly closer until his eyes are level with mine.

"Sure."

There. I said it. Surely Melanie and Lauren won't mind. Melanie even has a crush on Jamie, right? Maybe this will turn out perfectly. Maybe I could take a breather from over-thinking every little thing. Maybe my senior year of high school will actually be less than hideous. Except ...

"What?" Blake says, and I cringe at apparently being so transparent.

I shrug nervously. "You're sure you're up for a ... bonfire?"

Blake's face darkens, and my heart sinks.

"I didn't mean anything by—"

"It's okay," he says quietly. "It's just ... I thought maybe you were the one person who didn't know ... the one person in this school who wouldn't define me by ... "

My eyes prod him to continue, but he looks down in defeat and murmurs, "I guess that'll follow me the rest of my life."

I shake my head. "No," I insist. "I just happened to over-hear. I'm so sorry I mentioned it ... "

"Forget it," he says, finally meeting my eyes again. "I don't mean to sound so defensive. It's just ... you know, over two months have passed since it happened, and even though it's on my mind every second of the day, I've started thinking, 'Maybe I can finally move on.'"

"I get it, I get it," I assure him, oblivious to the students brushing past us on their way to class. "In fact, I don't just *get* it ... I *live* it."

Blake studies me closer. "What do you mean?"

I take a deep breath and offer my hand. "Tragedy Guy, meet Tragedy Girl."

He takes my hand, but simply holds it instead of shaking it.

"Perhaps you've heard," I say in response to his curious expression. "My parents died in a car crash last spring. That's why I'm here; I moved in with my aunt and uncle right before school started."

He squeezes my hand tighter. "I'm sorry."

I nod and swallow hard as Blake's index finger gently rubs the top of my hand.

"So I get it ... you know?" I say, pushing past the lump in my throat. "I don't want to be defined by my tragedy, either. I want to move on too. Not forget, of course ... just move on."

He lets my hand drop, then places his palm lightly against my cheek.

Our eyes lock for a second, but I look away when I realize someone is glaring at me. Natalie is walking toward me as she makes her way down the hallway, pressing her books against her chest and narrowing her dark eyes. I actually hear her huff as she scurries past me, deliberately jostling my arm. What the hell ... ?

"So, tonight," Blake says, clapping his hands together, seemingly oblivious to Natalie's shot of frigid air. "It's a date?"

I pause, then smile and nod.

I guess that clears one thing up:

It's a date.

Lauren and Melanie catch up with me as I head toward class. "Still coming with us to the bonfire tonight?" Melanie asks.

"Um..." I fidget with the rings under my shirt. "Sure. A couple of other people want to join us too, if that's okay."

They exchange stymied glances. "Who?" Melanie asks.

"Blake and Jamie? I hope that's okay. If it's not, I totally under—"

"*Jamie?*" Melanie says, her eyebrows widening. "Hells yeah!" She gives me a fist bump. "Girlfriend, we should have added you to our posse ages ago," she teases as we wind our way to our seats.

"Easy for you to say," Lauren grouses. "What am I, your chaperone?"

"Oh, I think Blake's brother is coming too," I say as we settle into our seats. "Not like it's a fix-up or anything. Really, guys, I hope this is okay. I totally didn't mean to take over your—"

"Garrett?" Lauren interrupts.

I shrug. "I don't know his name."

"Of course Garrett," Melanie says. "Blake only has one brother."

She turns toward me. "Lauren just broke up with her boyfriend," she says.

"Um, technically, I got dumped," Lauren clarifies. "His loss."

"You have to come with us," Melanie beseeches her. "You *know* I've been crushing on Jamie for months now—since even *before* he started lifting weights and got hot. And who knows? You might really click with Garrett."

Lauren shakes her head. "I don't want to be fixed up."

"Fine!" Melanie says, presenting the palm of her hand as an oath. "We'll just go as a group."

Lauren deliberates a moment, then says, "Whatever. I'll go. But *only* as a group. No pairing up and leaving me stranded with the junior."

"Absolutely," I say, feeling guilty that I seem to have commandeered their plans.

"Yes, fine, fine," Melanie says. "Anne, count us in."

I nod, then lean in closer. "That creepy Natalie girl practically shot daggers through me in the hallway," I tell them in a lowered voice. "What's up with her?"

"Hmmmm," Melanie says. "You were with Blake at the time?"

"Well, our lockers are right next to each other..."

"She's probably been planning her wedding to Blake since she started bringing him brownies all the time in middle school," Lauren says.

"He had cancer," Melanie says matter-of-factly. "Natalie apparently perceived that as a glass-half-full kind of opportunity."

"So, they've dated?"

Lauren snorts. "She wishes. I don't think Blake's ever dated anybody but Cara—the girl who died. I guess Natalie figured this was her chance. Then along comes Number Eleven..."

She and Melanie laugh at my perplexed expression. "Remember?" Lauren prods. "The guys have decided you're an eleven?"

I squeeze my eyes shut and shake my head.

Melanie peers into space. "Who knows, Natalie might have even offed that poor girl." She gives us a silly grin, then turns somber when she sees our reactions. "Alrighty then. Note to self: too soon to joke about dead girl."

Lauren swats Melanie's dark blonde hair playfully. "We are *so* signing you up for sensitivity training."

"Just don't schedule it for tonight," Melanie says. "Looks like I've got myself a date."

———

I shut the front door and take a deep whiff of pepperoni.

"Hi, honey," Aunt Meg calls from the kitchen. "Home-made pizza for dinner!"

"Yum," I say, walking into the kitchen. "Aunt Meg, I wish you wouldn't feel like you had to rush home from work and cook dinner for me. I'm fine fending for myself. And, you know, if you're not scared of botulism, I could start cooking for *you*."

She laughs, too loud, too hard. "Silly. Uncle Mark and I love cooking for you. And we were thinking maybe a movie after dinner?"

I hug my arms together. "It sounds great, only..."

"Yes?" Aunt Meg prods.

"I kinda have plans with some friends from school, if that's okay. There's a bonfire tonight to kick off the football season."

"Oh, honey, that sounds great! I'm so glad you're making friends. I knew it would happen in no time." Her eyes turn wistful. "Your mom and dad would be so happy."

The moment hangs in the air, then I say, "I dream about them a lot."

Aunt Meg intertwines her fingers. "You do?"

I nod. "I dream that I'm at some random place—a car wash, or a grocery store, wherever—and I glance over and there they are, in my peripheral vision. At first, it doesn't seem like any big deal...just, 'Oh, there are Mom and Dad.' But then I remember—in my dream, I mean—I remember they're dead, so I get super excited that I'm seeing them. I start rushing toward them, but they hurry away, hiding their faces. The more I call to them, the farther away they get."

I gaze into space, my eyes suddenly misty.

"It's so frustrating. I'm like, '*Please* come back.' But then I hear my mom's voice telling me it's too soon. It's too soon to see their faces; it'll just upset me. But I tell her it's not too soon, and that even if I get upset, who cares? I'd give my right arm to see them under *any* circumstances, even in a dream."

I swallow the lump in my throat. "You'd think I could at least see them in my dreams."

Aunt Meg sniffles and dabs at her moist blue eyes. "Oh, sweetie," she whispers in a choked voice.

I slip my hands into my jeans pockets. "I didn't mean to make you sad."

"No, no... I *want* you to talk to me. About your parents, about your dreams, about school... about everything."

Then she hugs me, smelling all fresh and floral, and I think fleetingly, *Who knows. Maybe I can.*

Maybe this is a start.

SIX

Blake tosses a candy wrapper into the bonfire and we watch it crackle and burn, our fingers dangling over our knees.

We got here late, opting for an impromptu frozen yogurt run, so the crowd has largely dispersed. People are still milling around on the football field, chatting with friends, sipping Cokes, or pouring some rum into their cups after surreptitious glances for chaperones. This is an official school function, after all, but even the adults seem mellow on this balmy starlit evening, a sea breeze occasionally wafting through the air from the Atlantic Ocean a few blocks away.

The six of us are sitting on a blanket: Blake, his brother Garrett, Jamie, Melanie, Lauren, and me. The vibe has been totally casual all evening—just a group of friends hanging out, although Melanie is subtly amping up the flirting with Jamie. A few guys have exchanged daps with Blake and offered him the obligatory pity smiles I've grown to know so well, but they're otherwise giving him a respectful distance. No wonder Blake was ravenous for a friendship with no baggage. Being pitied is exhausting.

"Man, toss me a piece of gum," Blake tells Jamie.

All eyes fall expectantly on Jamie, who pretends he didn't hear.

"*Dude*," Blake says.

Jamie's eyes flicker in his direction. "*What?*" he says.

Blake pauses a beat, then says, "Gum. Toss me a piece of gum?"

A long moment passes before Jamie reaches into his jeans pocket and produces the stick of gum. He holds on to it for a moment, then finally tosses it to Blake, his face inscrutable. He picks up a nearby stone and tosses it into the embers with a quick flick of his wrist.

I'm so confused. This is the friend who, I'm told, practically worships Blake? The sidekick who's happy to bask in his way-more-popular friend's afterglow? Jamie's behavior doesn't compute at all. He acts like he *despises* Blake. Or resents him. Yes, definitely resents him. I guess that makes sense; he was probably happy for Blake to call all the shots in the friendship when he was a scrawny, invisible little nobody, but now that he's a ripped River Phoenix look-alike, he's no longer interested in settling for Blake's scraps. Is that what's going on here? But it just seems so insensitive, given what Blake has gone through. I mean, it's easy enough to hate the best-looking guy in school, unless he happens to be a cancer survivor whose girlfriend just died.

"So . . . I heard about your folks," Garrett tells me, sneaking a glance at me. "It's . . . just awful. I'm so sorry."

I smile at him. "Thanks."

"I can't imagine *one* of my parents dying, let alone both of them at the same time," Melanie says.

"Yeah," I say. "Sucks."

Silence.

"Didn't mean to bring everyone down," I murmur, but then I look up brightly. "You know what? There's an upside. When life throws you the biggest curve ball you can imagine, you realize you're stronger than you thought you were. You realize you're a survivor."

More silence, and now my eyes dart anxiously from one face to the next. Was that the wrong thing to say? I mean, considering that Blake's girlfriend *wasn't* a survivor? The guys are all staring at their hands, but Melanie and Lauren offer supportive smiles.

"That's a good thing to know about yourself," Lauren says.

I suck in my lips as I realize a tear is rolling down Jamie's cheek. Melanie notices too, and she moves in closer. "You okay?"

He nods, rubbing his cheek roughly with his fist.

"Dude," Blake says quietly.

"*What?*" Jamie snaps at him, making us jump.

Blake's palms fly in the air. "Nothing, dude, nothing. Just trying to be supportive. We're cool . . . okay?"

Jamie holds his gaze, his eyes tear-stained but steely.

My mind reviews the information I've learned about Cara's death: some friends were at a bonfire, Cara took off for a late-night swim, Blake and Jamie jumped on a jet ski and took off looking for her when they realized she was in trouble...

Right. Blake and Jamie. This was Jamie's tragedy too. And yet he's probably been barely an afterthought in people's minds. It was Blake's girlfriend, Blake's loss, Blake's heartache. Once again, Jamie was relegated to sidekick. Maybe that's where all this hostility is coming from...

"Oh. My. God."

We all glance up and see Natalie staggering toward us, the contents of a plastic cup sloshing in her hand.

"Hi, Natalie..." I say.

"You really did it," she says, her words slurred. "You dragged this poor guy to a bonfire. Brilliant, new girl, brilliant." She juts out her chin. "Well, let me tell *you* something, Miss All-That: you don't breeze into town messing with *my friends*. Got it?"

"Natalie, what are you—"

"You don't have to defend her, Blake," Natalie tells him, her tone shrill. "I know a conniving bitch when I see one."

Garrett jumps to his feet and faces her. "Time for you to move along, Natalie."

"Oh, please! She's got you snowed too?" she asks Garrett, her words thick and sloppy. "You, of all people? Nobody knows better than you how devastated Blake is. You too, Jamie. A real friend would protect him from some slut trying to move in on him when he's still totally—"

"Go home, Natalie!" Garrett snaps. "You're drunk."

Two girls timidly approach her from behind and start pulling her arms.

"No!" Natalie protests, shaking them away. "I won't let my friend get his heart broken all over again." She locks eyes with Blake. "I care about you!"

The girls are pulling her harder now, but Natalie breaks free again.

"You don't even know for sure that she's dead!" she tells Blake. "I mean, they never found her body, right?"

She jerks around toward me. "The love of his life might still be alive, you moron! Still think it's a cool idea to throw yourself at him? Just because you look like Cara doesn't mean you can step right into her life. And stop boring everybody with *your* sob story, by the way. Yes, everybody's heard by now, Anne. Dead parents? Whatever. Parents are *supposed* to die before their kids. It's not the same thing as what Blake is going through at all. *You leave my friend alone!*"

Now, all three guys are on their feet. When Jamie reaches for Natalie's arm, she splashes her drink in his face. "Some friend you are."

The plastic cup falls from her limp hand as Jamie wipes the drink from his face. Her friends start pulling her insistently, and Natalie, now heaving throaty, jagged sobs, reluctantly lets herself be dragged away.

Everyone is frozen in place for a solid minute. The guys stay on their feet, the girls and I sit stunned and saucer-eyed on the blanket.

It's Blake who finally shakes us from our stupor by

throwing his hands in the air. "What the hell ... I hardly even *know* that lunatic!" he sputters.

"I knew she was an idiot, but I didn't know she was unhinged," Lauren says, her voice somber.

The guys exchange charged glances.

"Oh, Anne ... " Melanie says. "I can't believe what she said about your—"

"It's okay, it's okay," I say.

"But to talk about your *parents* that way ... " Melanie mutters, her words trailing off.

"I barely even know her!" Blake repeats, clenching his knuckles as a vein bulges in his neck.

Jamie studies him evenly. "Yeah, well, she sure as hell knows you."

"So ... *that* was fun."

Blake drops his head and laughs sheepishly. He's dropped off everyone besides his brother and is lingering at my aunt and uncle's front door, occasionally swatting a moth as it dives for the porch light.

"I dare that psycho to ever speak to me again," he says. "Or to you."

I wave a hand breezily through the air. "Aw, I've been through worse," I say. "A girl in second grade cut off my braid one day in art class. True story. Although ragging on me for having dead parents ... that's a close second."

Blake's closed-mouth smile is showcasing a dimple I've never noticed. I squelch the impulse to reach out and touch it.

"Let me make it up to you," he says. "Dinner tomorrow? I know Jamie had a good time with Melanie; we could make it a foursome."

My eyebrows arch. "That was Jamie having a good time?"

Blake shrugs. "He's just a little...edgy lately. But he's a good guy. Really."

He snatches my hand and kisses it. Then he leans in and kisses my lips.

It's crazy...I barely know him.

But suddenly, kissing him back feels like the most natural thing in the world. His lips are warm and salty, like the sea air. He presses me tighter as I kiss him back. I love the feel of his arms around me, strong yet gentle. We kiss for a long moment—his head tilting right while mine tilts left, then vice versa—before we reluctantly pull away.

That's when I glance at the driveway and notice Garrett looking at me from the front seat of Blake's car. I clear my throat and point discreetly at the car.

"Your brother..." I say.

Blake smiles his dimpled grin. "Yeah, I'll definitely leave him home tomorrow night," he says.

I smile back, yet feel a chill run up my spine. I can't quite shake the look I just saw on Garrett's face when I pulled away from Blake. Yes, having Garrett share our private moment was clearly awkward, but his expression registered something else as well. What did I see in his eyes as he watched me kiss his brother? Worry? Concern? Protectiveness? Yes, all those things. But it was the underlying emotion that made me shiver.

I saw fear in his eyes.

Uncle Mark is reading a book on the couch when I walk in.

"Hi," I say, straightening my shirt.

He puts his book aside and sits up straighter. "Hi, honey. Have fun at the bonfire?"

I nod, feeling my cheeks flush as my mind races anxiously. From this vantage point, Uncle Mark couldn't have seen Blake kiss me on the doorstep . . . right? And so what if he did? Is it a crime to kiss a guy on the doorstep, even after knowing him only a week? Still, it seems so . . . frivolous. My parents just died, for crying out loud. His *girlfriend* just died. Christ!

"I'm glad you're making friends," Uncle Mark says, seeming to intuit my thoughts. "It's what your mom and dad would want."

Would they? Would *they* be okay with my kissing a guy I barely know? Especially a guy who's so . . . I dunno . . . complicated? Or are our mutual tragedies the ingredients that are somehow drawing us together, that make it right for us to be together? I don't know, I don't know, I don't know . . . It's just that nothing feels quite right anymore. Everything seems somehow . . . off.

Quit overthinking, I snap to myself.

"You know, your parents met in high school," Uncle Mark says.

I nod and settle into a chair. "I know. Partners in the frog-dissecting lab."

"The formaldehyde fumes must have jumbled your mom's brains," Uncle Mark teases. "Otherwise, your dad wouldn't have stood a chance. She was *so pretty*. Just like you."

I smile, staring at my lap.

"And she was so smart," Uncle Mark continues. "Always way more mature than the other girls. She just had kind of this way about her ... very confident and self-assured, even though she never seemed snobbish or anything. She just kinda ... knew who she was and felt really comfortable with herself. You don't see that every day in a teenager."

I nod wistfully.

"Again," Uncle Mark said, pitching forward in his seat, "*just like you*,"

I can't meet his eyes. "That's not like me at all," I say softly.

"It is, honey," he insists earnestly. "You are the most together girl I know ... even after what you've been through."

Then why do I feel so confused? I ask myself. *Why can't I get my bearings?*

I just can't quite wrap my head around how I feel about Blake.

And I can't get Garrett's expression out of my head.

SEVEN

"That was the craziest thing I've ever seen." Melanie taps her straw idly. "I mean, I knew Natalie was screwy, but—"

Blake signals for the waitress. "Coke refill, please?" The waitress nods and grabs his empty glass, then heads toward the back of the restaurant with it.

"I knew she had a crush on you, but who knew she was, like, psycho?"

I roll a bit of paper from my straw between my fingers and bite my bottom lip. Granted, Natalie's meltdown last night was legendary, but I wish Melanie would change the subject. Can't the four of us just have a fun, relaxing evening? Maybe talk about the movie we just saw?

"Hey, did any of the rest of you notice the preview for the horror movie during the—"

"And what's *really* weird," Melanie says to Blake, "is that she acts like the two of you have some kind of a past. Like she was your girlfriend or something."

Blake snorts. "In her dreams."

My heart sinks a little. I'm not about to start a fan club for Natalie, and I totally understand Blake's bitterness about the way she acted, but she's clearly a troubled, insecure girl. What's the point in taking potshots?

"She is *delusional*," Melanie agrees, the word rolling on her tongue.

"A total wacko," Blake says, smiling at the waitress as she returns with a filled glass.

"Please," Jamie mutters under his breath.

Blake levels a steady gaze at him. "What's that supposed to mean?"

Jamie's eyes skitter away, but then he meets Blake's gaze. "It means don't act like you don't love the attention," he says, jerking his head to toss his blonde hair from his face.

Blake's eyes narrow. "Love the attention? Love a girl coming up and throwing a tragedy in my face?"

"She wasn't throwing it in *your* face," Jamie corrects him, his voice unsettlingly soft. "She was throwing it in *our* faces."

"So creepy that Cara's body was never found ... " Melanie muses, more to herself than anyone else.

Jamie's eyes fall, and Melanie finally notices the tension. She touches Jamie's arm. "I'm sorry," she says. "I know this is a terrible memory to dredge up." She looks at Blake. "I'm really sorry."

The moment hangs in the air, then Melanie asks Blake, "So ... how long did you two date?"

Blake rubs the back of his neck. "Can we change the subject, please?"

Melanie blushes. "Yeah, sure. In fact ... " She takes Jamie's hand. "Wanna play pool, Jamie?" She nods toward the poolroom in the back.

Jamie and Blake share another glance before Jamie nods ever-so-slightly. "Okay," he says.

"Mmmm ... bathroom first?" Melanie says to me, which I guess is my cue to accompany her.

The guys step out of the booth to let us pass, and Melanie and I head to the restroom.

"Sorry," she tells me as we go inside. "I've never been in this kind of situation before. My natural instinct is apparently to blab incessantly."

I smile. "It's okay. I guess you have to feel your way along. Hey, Mel?"

She glances at me as the door closes behind us. "Yeah?"

"Why do you think Jamie is so hostile to Blake?"

She leans into the mirror over the sink to touch up her lipstick. "I dunno, but I see now what you're talking about. It's a whole new vibe for them. They used to be total goofballs ... very light-hearted. I guess the drowning really did a number on them."

I shake my head. "But why would Jamie be *mad* at Blake?"

Melanie shrugs, pressing her lips together and tossing

her lipstick tube back in her purse. "I don't know that he's *mad* . . . more like on edge."

"That's what Blake said," I say. "That Jamie's been really edgy since the tragedy. Understandable, I guess . . ."

Melanie spins on a heel to face me. "Well, good news: I intend to do everything in my power to help Jamie relax. *God*, he's hot. Think it's premature to post pictures of us together on Facebook?"

"Um . . ."

"Too late. I already did. Don't you think he's cute?"

"Yeah," I say.

"There's something so . . . *vulnerable* about Jamie. I think I'm in lust."

I squeeze my arms around my chest. This is all so new to me, since I always steered clear of banal chatter about alpha males and Facebook photos. With Sawyer as my best friend, I enjoyed a comfortable and, okay, somewhat condescension-filled distance from the angst and drama of high school, even when I was dating someone. Now I feel I've been thrust into a leading role. A little exhilarating, I guess—Blake is definitely a hottie—but I can't help feeling like I'm playing a part. Add a poor girl's drowning as the backdrop, along with my own raw grief, and life has never felt more surreal.

"Well," Melanie says, "I'm outie. Will you tell Jamie I'll be waiting at the pool table?"

"Sure."

As she leaves, I glance at my own image in the mirror. *You're the most together girl I know*—Uncle Mark's words ring in my head. If only he knew how much clatter was in my head.

I exhale through puffed-out cheeks, open the bathroom door, and head back for our table. As I get close, I hear Blake talking in a tight voice to Jamie: "Just *cut it out*, for god's sake."

I can't hear Jamie's response, but Blake replies, "Don't go there. Just change the subject. You've got to stop letting…"

Jamie spots me first, and Blake's gaze follows his.

I finger the rings under my shirt. "Melanie's waiting for you at the pool table," I say.

Jamie blushes, nods, and walks away. For some reason, I take his seat rather than scooting back in next to Blake in the booth.

"That sounded kind of intense," I say, figuring it would be more awkward to ignore the tension than to point out the obvious.

Blake nods, his expression dark and brooding. "I keep telling him we have to move beyond the drowning," he says. "Just because other people bring it up doesn't mean we have to talk about it. It just keeps him really stirred up."

I lean into the table. "I don't get why he acts mad at you," I say.

Blake considers my words, then shakes his head bitterly. "I think he feels like I didn't do enough to help her."

I gasp a little. "That's terrible. How dare he make you feel like that."

Blake shrugs. "Why shouldn't he feel that way? *I* do."

I reach across the table for his hand, and he lets me hold it. "Don't do that to yourself," I say in a hushed voice. "Don't beat yourself up with guilt."

Blake's chin quavers and his blue eyes fill with tears.

"Oh, Blake..."

"Jamie was right there," he says in a trembling voice. "He knows what happened. There were so many things I did wrong. Why did I let her take a swim that time of night? If I couldn't talk her out of it—and no, by the way, I didn't even try—then why didn't I go with her? Why did I wait so long to go look for her? And did I try hard enough? Could another five minutes on the jet ski have made a difference?"

I rub his hand with my thumb. "Stop it," I whisper. "It was just a terrible accident."

He swallows hard, then looks at me, his eyes still misty. "That's what I tell Jamie. He acts like he's mad at me, but I think he's really mad at himself. He feels guilty too."

I shake my head briskly. "There's no place for anger or guilt in all of this. Blake, listen to me: I felt guilty after my parents died. What if I'd made dinner that night so they wouldn't have gone out? What if I'd gone with them? They asked me to. And, you know, I could have made them wait an extra five minutes while I got ready, or wait while I ate dessert—any single variable could have changed everything. A single *instant* could have changed everything, and I'd still have my parents."

He squeezes my hand and touches my cheek with his index finger.

"I think we need to let go of all the what-ifs," I say. "I think it's time to cut ourselves some slack."

Blake gazes into my eyes. "You're amazing," he tells me, and a deep sense of calm washes over me.

Maybe this *is* real. Maybe it's right.

"Why do you sound so giddy?"

I huff playfully. "Quit peering into my soul, Sawbones. It's annoying."

"Oh my god. It's that guy, isn't it?"

Okay, I haven't so much as *mentioned* Blake, even though he just dropped me off and I still have the warm, salty taste of his kisses on my lips.

"Did you see him tonight?" Sawyer asks.

I roll my eyes. "So what if I did?"

"Just seems like things are moving kinda ... fast. You said this year was going to be all about school and getting positioned for good scholarships. Since when did your college goals take a back seat to some guy?"

I huff. "You make it sound like some childish, shallow relationship," I say, then curse myself for uttering the word "relationship." "It's not like that at all. Blake and I have both been through a lot. We understand each other."

"Hmmmm," Sawyer says.

"But just to put your mind at ease," I say, "it's not like we're planning to elope. That whole college scenario? I've still got that penciled in."

I expect him to crack wise, but instead he says, "I really hope so, E. I don't want you getting off track."

I toss my head back as my jaw gapes. "Oh my gosh, I barely know him!"

"Yet you mentioned something about a relationship," Sawyer says, and I groan aloud.

"Please trust me," I tell him solemnly, irritated and yet a little touched as well.

"I trust you implicitly, E," he says. "Guys, on the other hand—"

"Hey, Sawbones, somebody's buzzing in. Catch you later?"

"Catch you later," he says.

I press a button on my phone. "Hello?"

"Anne?"

"Yeah?"

"It's Melanie."

I sit up straighter. Why does she sound so strange? "Is everything okay, Mel?" I ask, pressing a finger against my lip.

"Something's weird," she says, her voice a chilling monotone.

"What? Did something happen with Jamie?"

"No," she says. "At least I don't think so. I'm not sure what's going on."

I pitch slightly forward on my bed. "What?"

Melanie takes a deep breath. "When Blake and Jamie dropped me off tonight, I noticed the flag was up on my mailbox. I thought that was odd—the flag up on a Saturday night? So I looked inside."

I swallow. "Yeah?"

"There was an anonymous note in there," Melanie says.

I clutch the phone tighter. "What did it say?"

"It says: *Rethink your love life. Please. Your life may depend on it.*"

"*What?*"

"And the last sentence is underlined, Anne: *Your life may depend on it.*"

EIGHT

"Okay, let's just think this through."

Melanie paces in her bedroom, running her hand through her hair.

"It's got to be Natalie," I say, sitting cross-legged on her carpet as crepe myrtle branches rustle outside her bedroom window.

"But Natalie's hung up on *Blake*, not Jamie," Melanie says, repeating the same argument she made last night on the phone yet shaken enough to regurgitate the precious little information we have at hand. "Why would she care who Jamie's dating?"

I rest my chin on my knuckles. "You said yourself she likes to call dibs on *all* the guys—that even if they're not interested in her, she doesn't want them being interested in anybody else, either," I say. "And Jamie's transformation into a stud surely hasn't gone unnoticed."

Melanie stops pacing and catches my eye. "That means it hasn't gone unnoticed by Blake, either."

My eyebrows crinkle. "What do you mean?"

Melanie taps her index finger against her thigh. "Jamie was always a little nobody, just Blake's hanger-on. His wannabe. Maybe Blake's not taking it so well that Jamie's finally getting some attention."

"*What?* How insecure do you think Blake is? Besides, guys don't even care about that kind of stuff, do they? And, uh, there's that little detail of Blake being with us all night...including when the letter was placed in your mailbox."

"I mean, he could have had somebody put it there for him..." Melanie says, then glances at me for a quick sensitivity check. She walks over and sits next to me on the floor. "Hey, Anne, I'm not ragging on Blake. I think he's a really nice guy, and I agree, this doesn't seem like a guy move at all. I'm just trying to think everything through. And like you've been saying, there's some heavy-duty tension between Blake and Jamie these days."

Melanie's mom creaks open the door and peeks in. "You girls doing okay?" she asks. Melanie nods impatiently, prompting her mother to close the door again and leave us alone.

"Blake explained that to me last night," I say. "He thinks Jamie blames him for not saving Cara, or, I don't know, not trying harder...something like that. But he thinks Jamie is mostly just mad at himself. There's a lot of guilt there. Both of them feel guilty."

Melanie nods. "I know. I feel like Jamie and I are getting

along okay, but there's a wall there, you know? He just seems so...wounded."

I peer into space. "I just thought of something else weird."

"What?" Melanie prods.

"It's probably nothing, but...do you think Lauren and Garrett are pissed that they weren't invited last night?"

Melanie contemplates the question. "It's possible. Lauren actually had fun with Garrett Friday night—at least when Natalie wasn't spazzing out on us. She was hoping he would ask her out, but she thinks the chances are low. She said he doesn't seem interested. He seems kinda...preoccupied. Like Jamie. I guess that girl's drowning really did a number on everybody."

"Speaking of Friday night," I say. "After the bonfire? Garrett was in the car when Blake walked me to the door. We...kissed. And when I pulled away, I saw Garrett looking at me. He looked...I dunno, worried, or concerned or something. It kind of creeped me out. The look in his eyes...it was really intense."

"You think Garrett planted the note?" Melanie asks. "But again, that theory leads back to *Blake*, not Jamie."

I shake my head. "I don't know. I don't know what to think."

Melanie taps her fingertips on the carpet. "I can't help thinking it has something to do with the dead girl."

We sit there for a moment, then Melanie's eyes sparkle mischievously. "Maybe it *was* the dead girl," she says. "The one whose body was never found?"

Whatever expression I get on my face makes Melanie wince. "Oh, right...too soon for dead-girl jokes. Sorry."

We sit quietly for another minute, and then I ask, "So, are you going to tell Jamie about the letter?"

Melanie shrugs. "I don't even know if he'll ask me out again. Like I said, he acts awfully ... distracted. Hey, maybe *he* slipped me the note. I guess that's one way to dump somebody."

"Blake mentioned the four of us going out again next weekend."

Melanie raises an eyebrow. "Did he now. Quite the take-charge kind of guy, no?"

I feel my cheeks flush.

"I was kidding," Melanie says. "Didn't mean to insult your sweetie."

Now my face feels hotter than ever. How stupidly presumptuous of me to act like Blake and I are some kind of *couple*. I barely know him! Sawyer's right: I'm not acting like myself at all. First, I'm gushing over some guy I barely know, and now I'm having a gossipfest with a girl (who, let's face it, I barely know either) about a drama-filled note. I was more mature than this in *middle* school. I hardly know these people at all, and worse, I'm starting to feel like I hardly know myself anymore.

"I'm feeling a little sick to my stomach," I tell Melanie, managing a weak smile. "I better head back home."

Home. Yet another dubious concept.

I wonder if I'll ever feel at home anywhere again.

———

"*Hey, beautiful.*"

The text is from Blake. He's sent me several today, probably half a dozen just since I got back from Melanie's house, but I've responded to only a couple of them, and then as tersely as possible. It's almost midnight, I've been studying for an English Lit test for hours, I have a shrink appointment after school tomorrow, I need some sleep…

But maybe these are just excuses. The note Melanie got really shook me up. It's one thing to stumble through life when nobody is paying attention, but *this* situation… I know it's not Blake's fault, but what with Natalie's outbursts and the creepy anonymous note and my general sense that Blake is the most talked-about person in school, I feel like a monkey in a zoo, being observed, monitored, scrutinized—the same feelings that drove me four states away after my parents died. It just feels like a lot of pressure.

"*Talk to me, babe.*"

I stare at the text, nibble a fingernail, and then respond: "*Been studying all day. Sorry I'm not very chatty.*"

He texts back: "*I'm lying in my bed crying.*"

I push myself up onto an elbow. "*Crying? Why?*"

"*A movie on TV tonite, this sappy movie about these star-crossed lovers. I saw it at the theater a few months back.*"

"*With Cara?*" I probe.

"*Yeah. Stupid, huh?*"

I stare at the words for a few seconds, take a deep breath, and then call him.

"Hey, babe," he says in a choked voice, sniffling.

"Hey. I hate that you're upset. I'm sorry; I didn't know…"

"I'm okay," he says, weeping through his words. "I'm much better now that I'm talking to you. I think I spent three solid hours at her gravesite today."

"I get it. Really, I do."

"Do you? Because, Anne, I want you to know, I think you're... I think you're maybe the greatest girl I've ever met." More sniffles. "I don't want to blow this by spending all my time with *you* talking about *her*."

"No, no, not at all. I'd think something was wrong with you if you *didn't* feel this way."

"I get that about you," he says, his voice still quavering. "You're so sensitive. Plus, you've been there. You *know*."

"Yeah. I know..."

"Well... I'm not going to spend the rest of my life blubbering. I'm going to devote my future to honoring her past. That's the least I can do." He chokes on his words.

"That's great, Blake."

"I mean it," he stresses. "I already do a lot of volunteer work for the children's hospital—that's where I was treated for my cancer, you know—and I'm told I'm really good at motivating and inspiring people. I'm going to devote my life to doing good. For Cara's sake."

I nod. "That's really admirable."

"But I'm not going to live in the past. Am I selfish for wanting to move forward?"

"No, of course not."

He sniffles some more. "I want to move forward, Anne. I want to move forward with you."

NINE

"I keep having these dreams."

"Yes?" Dr. Sennett says, a pencil resting against her chin.

I push my sweater tighter against my chest, chilled by the artificial air in her office. "I dream I catch a glance of my parents, then rush toward them, but then they're gone. I know they can't be far—I *just saw them*—but every street I take, or every door I go through, just gets me more off track. They get farther away instead of closer."

Dr. Sennett nods inscrutably, her brown hair resting on her shoulders.

"The weird thing," I continue, "is that I feel like I'm actually communicating with my mom while this is happening. She's telling me it's too soon to see them, that seeing them now, while my grief is still so raw, will only leave me upset and frustrated."

Dr. Sennett smiles mildly. "Sounds like a wise mom."

"But she's wrong," I say firmly. "I need to see them."

Dr. Sennett leans up, resting her forearms on her legs. "Anne, I don't delve too deeply into the supernatural, but just because you don't see them doesn't mean they're not there. The love and guidance they gave you while they were living? That's still here. They're still guiding you, if in no other way than through the seeds they planted while they were raising you. Can you be content knowing they're still a part of you without having to actually see them? At least for now?"

I blink briskly, surprising myself by having tears in my eyes. "I'm just so lonely..."

The clock on Dr. Sennett's wall ticks off the seconds. She plucks a tissue from a nearby box and hands it to me. I dab at my eyes.

"Can you make a little room in your heart for your aunt and uncle to pick up where your parents left off?" she asks quietly. "Can you do that, knowing that's what your parents would want?"

I smile ruefully. "My Aunt Meg is nothing like my mom."

Dr. Sennett nods, then asks, "Does she have to be?"

Yeah, she kinda does. No offense, Aunt Meg, but my mom was amazing—funny and whip-smart and ironic and quirky. She couldn't do perky if her life depended on it.

"In a way, maybe it's better that she's *not* like your mom," Dr. Sennett continues. "No ambiguity or divided loyalty there, right? Plus, the ways that she's different might add things to your life that you'll end up valuing, even if you can't appreciate them right now."

I dab my eyes some more. "But you don't understand," I say. "Aunt Meg and I don't have a real relationship; we're just cordial to each other. Don't get me wrong; I appreciate so much what she and Uncle Mark have done for me—in fact, I feel like every moment of my life has to be a testament to my appreciation. It's exhausting. There's nothing authentic about a relationship where you're constantly prostrate with gratitude."

Dr. Sennett fingers a lock of her hair. "What would you tell her if you weren't prostrate with gratitude? What would you share with her if your relationship was authentic?"

I think about the question, idly fingering my tissue. "I actually did tell her about these dreams the other day," I acknowledge. "She's a good listener. She's really sweet."

Dr. Sennett nods. "What else might you want to talk to her about? What else do you think your aunt could help you with?"

I think for a moment, then blurt impulsively, "I'd tell her I'm obsessed with a guy I met at school ... that he's crazy good-looking and seems really nice ... but that I'm not really sure if any of this is real or right, but then again, I tend to overthink every little thing, so ... "

Dr. Sennett smiles. "Sounds like you have a lot to share," she says. "Maybe your Aunt Meg is the right person to share it with. Maybe your mom is pulling some strings for you."

I squeeze my eyes shut self-consciously. "This is *so* not

me," I assure her. "I've never been boy-crazy or silly or super-ficial..."

"So this feels silly and superficial to you?"

I shrug. "Actually, it feels like the opposite. I know it *sounds* silly and superficial—that's why I'm so self-conscious about it—but I think the reason this guy and I are bonding is that we're both grieving. His girlfriend drowned over the summer. I think we *get* each other...you know?"

Again, Dr. Sennett's face is unreadable, but her eyes prod me to continue.

"Yet all this is taking place in high school, which means there's a lot of silliness all around us," I say. "This one poor insecure girl is totally threatened by me, and she made a scene at a bonfire over the weekend...then I think she left my friend a creepy anonymous note in her mailbox. I was nice enough to Blake today in school—that's the guy—but I was kind of avoiding him at the same time, because I'm not sure I can han-dle all the drama. If it was just the two of us without all this attention focused on us, that would be one thing, but..."

"So what does your gut tell you?" Dr. Sennett asks. "Are you willing to push past the silliness to get to know him better? And keep in mind, although high school is definitely a micro-cosm, your life will always be subject to some degree of judg-ment and scrutiny. There's no living in bubbles on this planet."

"I get that," I say. "And yeah, I think I want to get to know him better. It's just, the silliness notwithstanding, I wonder sometimes...do I really even know him at all?"

More seconds tick away on the clock.

"I think that's what a relationship is about—getting to know somebody," Dr. Sennett says. "Maybe he'll be the love of your life. Maybe you'll look back six months from now and wonder, 'What was I thinking?' Maybe he's a prince; maybe he's a jerk. I think the trick is knowing you don't have to be able to peer into the future; you just have to trust yourself to make adjustments when you need to. Enjoy the ride, pay attention, and know when it's time to strap yourself in for the long haul … or time to step off."

I sweep my bangs off my forehead and look up at her shyly. "He asked me out again today," I tell her. "He wants to go out this weekend … another double date with his best friend and a friend of mine. All of our dates so far—well, *both* of our dates—have been with other people along."

"Even better," Dr. Sennett says smartly. "Never hurts to have a girlfriend's set of eyes for some objective feedback."

My stomach tightens, but I nod.

"Remember," she says as we wrap up our session, "you don't have to have your whole future carved out in the next fifteen minutes. You just have to trust yourself."

———————

Aunt Meg turns down the radio as she drives me home and glances at me with her peripheral vision.

"So … it went okay?"

I peer into the late-afternoon sun. "Yeah," I say. "It did. Thanks for arranging that, Aunt Meg. It was really thoughtful."

Her face brightens. "I'm so glad it went well, honey. Mark thought it might seem pushy to set up an appointment, but it always helps to talk things through, right?"

I smile. "Hey, Aunt Meg?"

"Yeah?"

"You know when I went out with friends a couple of times over the weekend?"

"Yeah?"

"Well...there's this guy I kinda like."

I can tell she's willing herself to under-react, which strikes me as touching.

"Yeah...?"

"His name is Blake," I continue. "We've only seen each other a couple of times—outside of school, I mean—but he's asked me out again this weekend, and I think I'm feeling pretty good about it."

Aunt Meg nods, her eyes still on the road. "So he's a nice guy?"

"Yeah," I say. "He seems really nice. More mature than the average guy, I think, because he's been through a lot."

"Oh?" Aunt Meg says, still committed to nonchalance.

"He had cancer when he was a kid, and then his girl-friend died over the summer."

Aunt Meg catches her breath. "Oh no!"

"She drowned," I say.

Aunt Meg steals a glance at me. "What was her name?"

"Cara."

Her eyebrows widen. "I work with her aunt at the insurance agency. That was huge news—so tragic. Her family was just devastated."

"So ... did you know Cara?"

She shakes her head. "No, but I know a lot about her. I think she and Blake dated forever. Her family was really fond of him."

I press my parents' rings against my chest. "So did they blame Blake at all? I mean, for the drowning?"

"Oh, *no*. They knew it was a terrible accident. In fact, they were really worried about Blake and the other kids being traumatized. I know they wanted him to speak at her funeral ... "

"I read a newspaper clipping," I say. "He was too upset to speak. So was his friend Jamie. They're the ones who went out on a jet ski looking for her."

She shakes her head some more. "So tragic."

I nibble at my nail, then ask, "Do you think it's weird I'm seeing him? I mean, so soon after the accident? Does it look insensitive?"

Aunt Meg thinks for a moment, then says, "I don't think it's insensitive ... just maybe a little more intense than you'd want to sign on to for at this point in your life. I mean, after everything both of you have been through ... "

"It's nothing serious," I stress.

"Well ... things like this can *get* serious pretty quickly. Would you be up for that?"

"I don't know," I say wistfully. "I just know I'm enjoying spending time with him."

She nods, then says, "Well, I'd love to meet him. Wanna invite him over for dinner some time this week?"

"You mean at your house?" I clarify.

"Um, actually I mean at *our* house," she says, then reaches over to playfully pinch my thigh.

I laugh lightly.

"Okay," I say. "Our house it is."

TEN

"Then I blew out my knee during the third game of the season last year, so that was the end of football for me."

Uncle Mark and Aunt Meg nod as they take bites of their lasagna.

"That's a shame," Aunt Meg tells Blake, "but it's incredible you've been so active. I mean, in spite of your health problems."

I swallow hard. I really have embraced Dr. Sennett's advice since meeting with her two days earlier, trying to make more room in my life for my aunt, but it's moments like this that make me cringe. Aunt Meg seems to have an unerring knack for putting her foot in her mouth. I'm mortified Blake thinks I go around blabbing about his past. But he pushes past the awkwardness good-naturedly.

"You mean my cancer?" he asks.

Aunt Meg nods, her eyebrows an inverted V. "I hope you don't mind that I mentioned it ... "

"No, no," he assures her, his blue eyes sparkling. "Yep, I had cancer, and yep, it was touch-and-go for a while. But once my doctors gave me a clean bill of health, I moved forward full steam ahead and never looked back, other than volunteering for cancer causes every chance I get. I'd spent enough time on the sidelines in hospital beds hooked up to IVs. I wasn't about to waste another minute."

"Very admirable," Uncle Mark says softly, dabbing his mouth with his napkin.

"Absolutely!" Aunt Meg agrees, hoisting her wine glass in the air. "You're obviously a very resilient young man. That, and overcoming your loss this summer ... "

I grit my teeth. But again, Blake is unflappable, game for whatever Aunt Meg wants to lob his way.

"That made cancer seem like a walk in the park," he says solemnly. "I pray for Cara's family every day. And I take flowers to her mother every Sunday. I guess that might sound a little corny, but ... "

"It's a lovely gesture," Aunt Meg says. "You know, I work with her aunt."

Blake's eyebrows crinkle. "Really ... "

"Cathleen Wexler?" Aunt Meg says, nodding. "Her mother's sister?"

"Right, right," he says, gripping his fork a little tighter. "Aunt Cathleen. Give her my love, won't you?"

Aunt Meg rests her chin on her folded hands. "Wow. You really *are* close to the family."

Blake holds her gaze, an enigmatic smile on his face. "I just tend to be very loyal to the people I care about."

He takes my hand and squeezes it lightly. I glance at Uncle Mark, who is peering at our enfolded hands. When he notices that I'm looking at him staring at our hands, he shakes his head lightly and looks away.

"So," Uncle Mark says. "Anyone up for dessert?"

———————

"You're sure?"

The crickets chirp as Blake and I sway gently on the front-porch swing after dinner. "I'm sure," I insist. "I've barely even passed her in the hall. I promise, Natalie is *not* harassing me."

And it's true. Maybe she was embarrassed enough by her scene at the bonfire to abort her campaign to keep me away from Blake. Or maybe she knows Melanie and I suspect her of writing the note—which would mean, of course, that she *did* write the note, or at least know about it. Yes, all signs are pointing to Natalie as the culprit, which gives me a huge sense of relief. It eliminates the creepy unknown factor, and it makes Natalie's behavior outrageous enough that maybe she's decided she went too far. The upshot is that she's leaving me alone. At least for now ...

"I want you to let me know if she bothers you," Blake says firmly. He stops the swing with the heel of his foot, then places his palm against my cheek. "I couldn't stand it if I thought our relationship was causing you pain."

Our relationship. When I used the word "relationship" during my phone conversation with Sawyer, I immediately wondered if I was delusional. Blake and I had only had two dates, for crying out loud. But now, as we're finishing up our third date, Blake's called it a relationship too.

Dr. Sennett's words echo in my head: *I think that's what a real relationship is about ... getting to know somebody.*

And when both parties agree it's a relationship, well ... that makes it pretty official, right? I mean, he's just voluntarily had dinner with my aunt and uncle. And he's already made plans for Saturday night, another double date with Jamie and Melanie, without really even asking if I was free, because it was just kind of *implied.* When your weekend plans are implied, well ...

Blake laughs at me, his eyes sparkling.

"What?" I say.

"What are you thinking about?" he asks, his palm still caressing my cheek. "I can just see those wheels turning in your head a hundred miles an hour."

I consider saying something witty or self-effacing, but opt instead for authenticity as our eyes study each other in the gauzy moonlight. "A relationship," I say softly. "You called our friendship, or whatever it is ... you called it a relationship. I guess I'm wrapping my brain around having a relationship with somebody I just met. Is it possible to feel this strongly about somebody you didn't even know existed a mere two weeks ago?"

He leans in and kisses me, a tender, languid kiss. "You've taught me the answer to that question," he says as he pulls ever-so-slightly away, our lips still touching. "I'm falling in love with you, Anne."

———————

" ... almost *too* smooth."

Uncle Mark and Aunt Meg blush as I walk into the kitchen, clearing my throat to signal my arrival yet still catching them off guard.

"Who's too smooth, Uncle Mark?" I ask him, genuinely intrigued to see my laid-back uncle suddenly seem so intense.

He tosses the dish towel to Aunt Meg, who busies herself threading it through the refrigerator handle.

"So Blake's already left?" Uncle Mark asks, shifting his weight.

I nod. "He just left." I bite my lower lip. "Is that who you were talking about? Blake?"

After a couple of seconds of watching Uncle Mark cast about for a response, Aunt Meg jumps in. "Blake is *wonderful*," she assures me. "Your uncle and I are both very impressed. It's highly unusual for a guy his age to be so ... *poised*, I think is the word Uncle Mark was looking for. It just caught us off guard, I guess. In a good way, of course."

She nods vigorously, apparently pleased with her word choice.

But Uncle Mark isn't nodding. He's just standing there looking … concerned. Aunt Meg's spin notwithstanding, he definitely wasn't giving Blake a compliment when I walked into the room.

Too smooth.

That's what he said.

ELEVEN

"Oh, you should come too!"

Lauren gives Melanie a level stare. "Right. There's nothing pathetic about *that*."

"You wouldn't be a third wheel," Melanie insists. "You could invite Garrett."

Lauren raises a hand. "You. Must. Stop."

Melanie picks up a chicken nugget and gives an exaggerated pout before popping it into her mouth. "I think he really likes you," she says, her mouth full.

"Based on how many times he's called me since the bonfire?" Lauren says. "Let's see... hmmmm, wait a second, I'm counting... Okay, got it: he's called me zero times. Go on your little double date. I'll sit home and crochet."

"So Blake ate dinner with your family last night?" Melanie

asks me as people rustle around us carrying their trays to or from their tables.

I pause for a minute. *Your family*. Yes, idiot. That's who Uncle Mark and Aunt Meg are. They're family.

"Yep," I say. "They wanted to meet him, and he was free, so ... "

"Wow," Lauren says. "Dinner with the fam. This is heating up pretty quickly."

I narrow my eyes quizzically. "*Too* quickly?" I ask them, genuinely interested in their opinions. "Is this weird?"

Melanie offers a breezy smile. "What would be weird about it?"

I ponder the question, then shrug. "He and Cara were so close. I think she's the only girl he ever dated, and only a few months have passed since she—"

"Hey, life goes on," Lauren says, then sips her iced tea through a straw. "I mean, I feel terrible about the girl, but you can't expect a guy to stay in mourning the rest of his life."

"Still," I say, "they were incredibly close. He takes flowers to her mother every Sunday."

"Well, *that's* adorable," Lauren says drolly, and my stomach clenches as I wonder what she's insinuating. I guess she sees the anxiety etched on my face.

"I didn't mean anything by it," she assures me. "It *is* adorable. It's very ... Blake-like. He's ... quite a guy."

I purse my lips. I've been hearing these things about Blake a lot, but the compliments always seem tinged with a little, I dunno ... sarcasm? What's that about? Is it that noteworthy for a guy our age to be so mature? Is decency so extraordinary that people don't really quite buy it? That's totally unfair. So Blake's not a typical shallow high school airhead. Sue him, for chrissakes.

"Truly, Anne, I didn't mean anything by it."

I feel my neck grow warm. "It's fine," I murmur.

A tense moment hangs in the air, then Melanie leans closer. "I told Lauren about the note."

What? We'd decided, that morning in her bedroom, to keep the note a secret. The last thing we wanted to do was fan the flames, intensify the drama, drag out the childishness—at least that's the last thing *I* wanted to do. We even floated the idea that Lauren might have *written* the note, though that's clearly a long shot. Yes, I know it's hard to keep a secret, but I'm cringing right now. What is Melanie *thinking*?

I stare at Melanie with my jaw dropped.

"Sorry, Anne," she tells me, "but it's too creepy not to talk about."

She reaches into her purse and takes out the note, smoothing the paper on her lap. I instinctively reach over and try to grab it, but Melanie moves it beyond my reach.

Lauren presses her lips together. "Uh, in the *first* place," she tells me in a steady voice, "I've already seen the note. Remember? And in the *second*, it's Melanie's note—not yours. Plus, Mel and I have been best friends since fourth grade, so ... there's that."

I feel my cheeks grow warm. Lauren's message is clear: *You're the newcomer to the group. Back off, bitch.*

"I'm sorry," I tell her. "I wasn't trying to keep anything

from you ... and I know it's not my note. I'm just really nervous about people being in my business ... *our* business, I guess."

Lauren holds her frosty gaze. "Mel's business."

"Right," I murmur. "Mel's business."

"Oh, girls, let's all kiss and make up," Melanie says briskly. "Don't we have enough enemies without you two going at it?"

Lauren is still staring at me. "I'm really sorry," I repeat in barely a whisper.

Melanie snaps us to attention. "Okay, let's focus," she says impatiently. "The question is, why would Natalie write the note when it's Blake she has a crush on?"

My eyes widen as I see Natalie approaching us as she makes her way to the lunch line. I hold my index finger to my lips. Melanie follows my line of vision, spots Natalie herself, then hastily refolds the note.

"So Blake will pick us up Saturday night around seven?" she says, aiming for nonchalant.

"Um ... "

She shoots me a get-with-the-program glance.

"Oh, right," I say haltingly. "He'll pick up Jamie and me, then we'll swing by your house, and—"

"Perfect," Melanie says, discreetly slipping the note back into her backpack just as Natalie walks past us. "Well, gotta go. If I get to my fourth-period class early, I'll have time to study for my quiz."

Lauren and I follow her lead, standing up and collecting our trays. After we put them on the conveyor belt, I lean closer to Lauren.

"Sorry again," I say in a lowered voice. "I'm just a little freaked out by this."

She gives me a level gaze. "I get that. But Mel and I . . . we go way back. We don't keep secrets from each other."

I nod, my eyes oozing remorse.

"Hey, no harm, no foul," Lauren says, then offers a smile.

As I smile back, I see Blake and Jamie heading into the cafeteria. Melanie sidles playfully up to Jamie, taking his hand as she looks at him coyly, her chin tilted down. Blake approaches me and kisses me on the cheek. "God, you look gorgeous," he whispers in my ear.

I smile, but then shiver as I notice a pair of eyes boring into mine from the lunch line.

Natalie is staring at me, a cold, hard stare. My lashes flutter for a second, but she's still holding her gaze.

"What is it?" Blake asks.

I shake my head and say, "Nothing," but he's already looking around. When his eyes lock with Natalie's, he sets his jaw and tenses his muscles.

"It's nothing, Blake," I say, but he's giving her a steely glare.

Only then does Natalie turn away and finish filling her tray. But she sneaks one last glance at me as I walk out of the cafeteria.

I duck my head and rush off to class, shuddering as my mind subconsciously matches Natalie's expression with the words on the note:

Rethink your love life. Your life may depend on it.

TWELVE

"I'm waiting."

I glance up at Blake and smile shyly. "Sure," I say. "I'd love to."

Only a day has passed since Natalie shot me her death glare in the cafeteria, and I'm still a little rattled. Blake's just asked me to join his family this Sunday for dinner ("*Your* turn for twenty questions," he gleefully informed me), and I feel terrible that my hesitation might have suggested a lack of enthusiasm.

"That sounds great," I continue, feeling slightly perkier after a quick scan of the hallway indicates Natalie is nowhere in sight. But then, the day is young...

"It's Natalie, isn't it," Blake says in a tight voice.

"*No.*"

"I saw the way she was looking at you yesterday," he says, hitting his locker door with the side of his fist.

"It's nothing, Blake. It's fine…"

Blake notices his brother walking by and takes him by the arm. "Hey, Garrett."

Garrett slows his stride. "Yeah."

"That psycho Natalie? She's still messing with Anne."

Garrett's eyes study mine. "What's going on?"

"Nothing," I assure him, shaking my head briskly. "She hasn't said a word to me since the bonfire. I guess she kinda gave me the evil eye yesterday in the cafeteria, but it's totally—"

"What's so weird is that I've never even given her the time of day," Blake says. "That girl means *nothing* to me."

Garrett eyes his brother warily. "Maybe that's the problem."

Blake huffs. "What's that supposed to mean?"

Garrett shrugs. "Remember how she was always visiting you in the hospital when you were sick? Always bringing you things? She even made that scrapbook for you…"

Blake tosses his head back and moans. "Who gives a crap?" he asks. "Lots of people did nice things for me when I was sick. Am I supposed to marry all of them?"

Garrett looks at me, and my eyes skitter away. I feel so awkward being pulled into this drama. Sure, I understand Blake's point—Natalie certainly wouldn't be my first choice of a friend, no matter how many brownies she baked for me— but my heart feels a slight stab as I imagine how much she must really care about him, and how his indifference must cut like a knife. Yes, she's a world-class flake, but Blake—*Blake* of all people—could certainly muster a bit of compassion for someone who's been so nice to him … couldn't he? I'm just not sure how I feel. Am I being hopelessly naïve, or is Blake being a bit harsh? All I know is that it's hard looking Blake or Garrett in the eye right now.

"I'm not saying you should marry her," Garrett tells his brother. "I'm just trying to sort out why—"

"Sorry, guys, but Anne and I have to go."

We all look at Melanie, who has just speed-walked to my locker and is now pulling me insistently away, her lips pinched into a taut straight line.

"What in the world … " I murmur as she leads me down the hall, huddling close to my side as we walk.

She leans into my ear to deliver the news:

"I got another note."

———————

Melanie shushes me when I gasp.

"What does it say?" I ask as we round the corner toward our first-period class.

"I'll show it to you when we get to our desks."

Our shoes click on the tile as we rush inside.

Melanie scans the room as we enter. "Good. We're the first ones here."

Even the teacher isn't here yet; the bell won't ring for another seven minutes or so. As we take our seats, Melanie reaches into her backpack and pulls out a piece of paper.

She hands it to me somberly. I hesitate for just a beat,

then take it from her and begin reading the neat, slanted cursive in dark-blue ink:

Melanie,

I'm sorry I freaked you out by writing you an anonymous note, and I'm sorry it had to be anonymous. If you understood the circumstances, you'd know why I can't sign this one either. I really do hate that. It's not my style.

I was hoping a minimum of words would get my message across the first time, but I see you didn't take my advice. I'm thinking of nothing but your best interests as I beg you to reconsider. Stop dating Jamie. I'll repeat what I said in the last note, because it's true: your life may depend on it. He's bad news. Worse news than you can know. The only reason I'm going out on a limb to tell you this is because I, unlike Jamie, care about people. Even though I don't know you, I don't want any harm to come your way. I vowed I would share this warning with anyone Jamie dated, so now I'm sharing it with you. Please listen this time so both of us can get back to our lives and I can stop freaking you out.

I slowly lift my head. Melanie is wide-eyed.

"Where did you get this?" I ask.

"It was in my locker this morning," she whispers, then presses a finger against her lips as she nods toward the handful of students filtering into the room.

"Natalie … ?" I whisper.

Melanie nods. "It has to be."

"But whoever wrote this says she doesn't know you."

"So you think Natalie's above lying?"

"I don't know what to think..."

"Lauren has second period with her," Melanie says. "She's going to pass her a question in a note so she can get a sample of her handwriting."

I'm tempted to protest—isn't there enough game-playing going on?—but I learned my lesson the day before. I don't get to call the shots in this deal. They're Melanie's notes, as Lauren so pointedly emphasized. We're clear now about that, if nothing else, since the writer calls both Melanie and Jamie by name. This really doesn't have to concern me at all... does it? I mean, of course I'm concerned for Melanie and Jamie, and of course I'm curious, but this is about *them*... right?

So why do I feel such a thud in my stomach?

———————

Lauren shakes her head. "They don't match at all."

Melanie and I lean closer to the two notes on the cafeteria table and peer intensely at them, our eyes darting from one to the other and back again.

"Make sure you keep them covered," Melanie tells me nervously, and I tighten the boundary of my arm.

We squint at them a few more moments, then I say, "Lauren's right. There's no way the same person wrote these two notes."

"But all she says in her note to Lauren is *Tuesday at*

10:30," Melanie says. "That's not nearly enough of a sample to compare the letter to."

"What was I supposed to do?" Lauren grouses. "Ask her if she could write the first chapter of *War and Peace* from memory? Somehow it seemed less suspicious to ask when our French test is."

"It's enough to tell the handwriting doesn't match," I say.

We sigh and lean back in our chairs, Melanie slipping the notes back into her backpack.

"It *has* to be her ... " Melanie says, more to herself than to Lauren and me. "People can fake their handwriting, you know."

"Was your locker locked?" I ask her.

"Please. That lock's probably been busted since my mother went to school here."

"So anyone could have put it there ... "

"But who else would have wanted to?" Melanie asks.

"Why would *Natalie* want to?" Lauren says, clicking her fingernails against the table. "It's like we've said all along: she's into Blake, not Jamie. Hasn't she made that painfully obvious by now?"

"She just likes to stir things up in general," Melanie says. "And messing with Blake's best friend would be kind of like messing with him ... by proxy."

"She doesn't want to *mess* with Blake, she wants to *marry* him," Lauren reminds us. "Anne's the one she's messing with—and in very non-subtle ways. She's not making any secrets of her feelings. Why sneak around?"

"But she overheard us yesterday when we were talking

about going out this weekend," Melanie say. "She was walking right past us when we were talking about it. Bingo: she has new information, so time to swoop in again ... right?"

"Let me see the note again," Lauren says, "the second one."

Melanie digs it out of her backpack, glances around surreptitiously, and hands it to her under the table.

Lauren studies it, then says, "It's folded like it was in an envelope."

Melanie nods. "It was. A sealed envelope."

"Was anything written on the envelope?"

Melanie shakes her head.

A moment passes, then Lauren asks me, "What are you thinking?"

"Who, me?"

"You look like you're thinking something important," she says, and I realize I've been peering into space.

I shrug. "I'm just starting to wonder if we're asking the right questions."

"What do you mean?" Melanie says.

"I mean, we're spending all this time wondering who wrote the note. Maybe what's more important is knowing *why*. We sure are giving the letter-writer a lot of attention. Maybe the person we should be focused on ... is Jamie."

THIRTEEN

"I don't think it's a good idea."

Melanie crosses her arms. "They're *my* notes, Anne," she reminds me, "not yours."

She holds an even gaze for a moment, then softens ever so slightly. "I didn't mean to sound snotty," she tells me, squinting into the late-afternoon sun as students amble toward their cars or buses in the school parking lot. "I know this is creeping you out too."

Still, Melanie was clearly stung when I suggested in the lunchroom that Jamie, not the letter-writer, was the person we should really be worried about. She's been kind of cold all afternoon, and now she's floating an idea that she knows I won't like: showing the notes to Jamie. *Jamie,* of all people. I feel terrible that I've cast aspersions on him—yes, I get that the letter writer is probably full of crap—but how can we not at least consider taking the notes at face value?

I tug on my backpack strap. "It's just ... I hate to give those stupid notes so much power. The writer is obviously trying to get a rise out of us ... well, out of *you*. If we start showing the notes to other people, it'll just fuel the flames. Why give her the satisfaction?"

"*Her*," Melanie repeats pointedly. "So you think it's Natalie too."

I sigh. "Okay, let's say it *is* Natalie. We already know she's a flake, so, duh, now we have more evidence. Big whoop. The important thing is that we also know she's harmless."

"*Do* we?" Melanie says, a hint of urgency in her voice.

I give her a level gaze. "She's the kind of person who brings brownies to guys in hospitals," I remind her. "She's insecure, not vicious."

Melanie sucks in her lips. "The things she said to you at the bonfire were pretty vicious."

I shake my head, a muggy breeze rustling through my hair. "Still, I don't think she's going to bring an Uzi to school if you don't break up with Jamie. She's just trying to create drama. Wouldn't we be playing right into her hands if half the school was suddenly talking about her ridiculous anonymous notes?"

A steady stream of students walks past us on the sidewalk.

"I'm not talking about showing the notes to half the school," Melanie says, whispering now. "I'm talking about showing them to Jamie. He deserves to know somebody is ragging on him."

My shoulders droop. "But if Jamie knows, then Blake will find out, and he's already upset about Natalie, so ... "

Melanie observes me coolly. "Jamie doesn't tell Blake everything."

My eyebrows knit together. "Doesn't he?"

"It's so insulting. Everybody acts like Jamie is just an extension of Blake. He's his own person, you know. An awesome person."

I look at her quizzically. "What's going on?" I ask her.

She shrugs. "Our whole lives don't revolve around *you* guys, you know."

I hug my arms together. "What do you mean?"

She gives me a sly smile. "I mean we kinda hooked up last night."

My jaw drops.

"Why are you so stunned?" Melanie asks. "We *are* dating, after all. It's not like we signed a contract to only hang out with you and Blake. Not that we don't like hanging out with—"

"Where did you see him?" I ask, my stomach muscles tensing as I mentally review the messages from the notes.

Melanie tosses her head jauntily. "I called him. I told him I didn't want to wait until Saturday to spend more time with him, that I'd been thinking about him since our pool game and couldn't get him off my mind. I really like him, Anne. I'm going for it this time."

"So ... he came to your house?"

She nods. "He picked me up and we went out for ice

cream. Then we sat in his car in my driveway for ... a *very* long time."

I bite my bottom lip lightly.

Melanie seems to be gauging my reaction. "I don't hook up with just anybody," she tells me defensively. "I mean it, Anne. I really like Jamie."

I nod, feeling my heart beat against my blouse.

"But we didn't even really ... *do* anything last night. I mean, we kissed—he's a great kisser—but when it got heavier than that, he ... "

A distant rumble of thunder churns in an otherwise sunny sky. "He what?" I prod.

Melanie's lashes flicker. "He ... started crying."

I shift my weight, slipping a hand into my jeans pocket. "Oh."

"He cried for a long time," Melanie says, a faraway look in her eyes. "I kept asking him why, but he wouldn't tell me. He just ... held me really tight. Like, *clutched* me, almost. It broke my heart to see him cry, but it was so touching. It was like he knew he was safe with me, knew he could let down his guard. I've never felt so close to a guy."

Melanie studies my face, then says, "Whoever wrote those notes is just messing with me, Anne. There's nothing dangerous about Jamie. He's the most gentle, sweet guy in the world. And he deserves to know somebody's spreading rumors about him."

Another rumble of thunder rolls, this one closer. "Are you going to see him tonight?" I ask her.

Melanie shakes her head. "He's going out of town overnight with his family. I'll show him the notes on our date tomorrow. And I think Blake should see them too. If it's Natalie, he'll know better than any of the rest of us how to handle it. *He's* the one she's obsessed with, after all."

I swallow hard, then nod reluctantly. "Okay," I say, wishing I could untangle the knot in my stomach.

I guess it gives me some reassurance to know that Melanie thinks Jamie is the world's sweetest guy. But I barely know him, and I have a nagging suspicion that Melanie might not know him as well as she thinks she does.

That letter writer might be unhinged, but she—she, he, whoever—definitely knows something about Jamie that we don't.

I can't help wondering what it is.

———————

I smile as I see my head bobbing out of the water, Mom and Dad on either side of me.

I'm about eight in the photo, and frothy waves are splashing all around us.

I smile wistfully as my finger traces the picture, the clock on my bedside table ticking in the stillness. I'm having a hard time falling asleep tonight—another friggin' note, for crying out loud—so for the first time since the accident, I'm lying in bed thumbing through a photo album, one of several Aunt Meg stacked on the bookshelf when I moved in.

The picture I'm gazing at was taken right here on Hollis Island during high tide. I always loved high tide the best, when the waves can sweep you ten feet in the air, then either carry you to the shore or crash mercilessly over your head. Part of the fun was never knowing whether you were going to be whisked along with the wave, feeling like you were flying on a magic carpet, or unceremoniously dunked into the sea, thrashed about like a hand towel in a washing machine. I was up for either scenario, and I always went back for more. The bigger the waves, the better. I loved the rough-and-tumble dance with the ocean.

Of course, back when the picture was taken, Mom and Dad were never more than an arm's length away. They loved the ocean too, loved pushing me through a wave or plucking me out of the water like a drowning rat.

Drowning.

I peer into space. What must it have felt like for Cara to drown that night? She must have felt so alone in the inky darkness. It's what I imagine Mom and Dad feeling like in their last moments, too. Even though they were together, I wonder how much fear they felt as they took their last breaths. Did they meet each other's eyes? Reach out for each other's hands? Could they comfort each other in their last moment of consciousness, or is dying inevitably a solo endeavor? Did they think about me? Were they scared? So many questions ... so many questions I'll never have the answers to. If only I could at least see them in my dreams ...

Too soon, my mom's voice intones. *Too soon.*

As I flip the page of the photo album, I feel a stab in my chest as I contemplate how simple my life used to be. Friends with purple hair, or impromptu suspensions for breaking the dress code with leopard-print leggings—that's as action-packed as my life was a mere three months earlier. Now . . . anonymous notes, evil glares in the hall, a tragic drowning. I wish I could reach into the picture and recapture my eight-year-old life.

I wince as I reflect that the common denominator in all of the drama is . . . Blake.

I wonder what Mom and Dad would think of him. They'd always been famously tolerant of even my quirkiest friends (Jade with the purple highlights, Caroline with her goth makeup, Sawyer with his snarky nonconformity), but they were shrewd judges of character as well. My weird friends suited them fine; my sketchy friends, not so much.

Maybe they'd jump for joy over a guy like Blake: a high-achieving, wholesome-looking guy who volunteers at the children's hospital. What's not to love?

Unless they would agree with Uncle Mark's assessment.

Unless they'd worry that he was too smooth.

I shut the photo album, put it on my bedside table, turn off my lamp, and push the covers under my chin, trembling slightly as the crickets chirp outside. I think Uncle Mark is just being overly cautious. After all, this parenting business is totally new territory for him. And I'm sure he feels extra protective of me, considering what I've been through. Mom and Dad would appreciate his vigilance, no doubt. But they'd also probably roll their eyes at his paranoia, assuring him that only the most neurotic parents overreact to teenage stuff.

Yes. That's what they'd do.

I think.

A tear courses down my cheek as I ponder how badly I wish they were here to ask.

FOURTEEN

"Refill, please."

Blake nods toward his empty glass, and the waitress scoops it up and carries it off.

"I say we take a break from movies for a while," he tells us, putting his arm around my shoulder in our booth. "Two stinkers in one week are enough to make me take up bowling."

Jamie ignores him, studying his menu while flicking his blond hair off his shoulder, and I ignore Melanie, who's desperately trying to catch my eye. I know, I know; she's dying to show the guys the notes. But I still object, on the grounds I laid out in the school parking lot. I get that this is her call. Fine. Whatever. But I'm going to prolong my drama-free evening as long as possible.

"And what was with those special effects?" Blake says.

"Geez, I could've done better with my Deluxe Whiz Kid chemistry set. I've seen bigger explosions in science class."

Jamie interrupts his menu-reading just long enough to briefly scowl at him.

Jesus! If Blake has decided a break from movies is a good idea, I'm close to suggesting that a break from double dates is a downright *stellar* idea. Whatever tension is festering between Blake and Jamie is clearly not a fleeting thing.

The waitress returns with Blake's filled glass, and he offers her a dimpled grin and a wink. Now Jamie is glaring at him. Blake's eyes flicker in his direction, then quickly look away.

"Hey," Blake says, "I've heard the cheesecake here is really—"

"I've got something to show you."

Melanie exhales through puffed-up cheeks as all eyes fall on her. "There. I said it."

The guys look at her quizzically. I cringe.

"What is it?" Jamie asks her.

Melanie scans our faces, then reaches into her purse and puts the notes on the table, smoothing them with the heel of her hand. Blake and Jamie lean in closer, squinting at the pieces of paper.

"This was the first one," she says, pointing to the pithier of the two. "It was in the mailbox when I got home from our date last Saturday."

The guys' lips move subtly as they read it, Blake tilting his head for a better angle.

"Then, this one was in my locker yesterday."

Just as the guys' eyes rest on note number two, Melanie

plucks it up and reads it aloud. As she somberly reads the last line—*Please listen this time so both of us can get back to our lives and I can stop freaking you out*—I notice that Jamie's face has turned ashen.

"I wasn't sure when I got the first one whether it was really meant for me," Melanie says in a slow, deliberate cadence. "But the second one mentions Jamie and me by name. Jamie is the one I should stay away from. My life supposedly depends on it."

She purses her lips and folds her hands on the table.

"I gotta...I gotta..." Jamie bolts from the table and runs to the restroom, his chalky face now tinged with gray.

"Oh my gosh," Melanie says, craning her neck to follow his path. "Blake, should you go after—"

"Why would you show him that crap?" Blake asks her bitterly, a vein in his neck bulging.

Melanie blushes. "What do you mean? Why wouldn't I—"

"Don't you know we've been inundated with that kind of bullshit since Cara died?" he says, spitting out every word.

"I...I..." Melanie stammers.

"Brilliant move," he tells her, his acrid sarcasm sending a shiver up my spine. "Jamie had just started to relax, just started to cut himself a little slack, and now..."

"Now *what*?" I ask in a tight voice. "All Melanie did was show him a couple of notes that mentioned him by name. She didn't do anything wrong."

Melanie bites a lip to steady her quivering chin as her eyes fill with tears.

Blake's dart from her face to mine, then back again. "I'm sorry," he says softly. "I didn't mean to upset you, Melanie."

A tense moment hangs in the air, then he faces me to repeat, "I'm sorry." I try to hold his gaze, my head cocked defiantly, but his eyes fall.

Melanie twists her fingers together on the table for a moment, then she bolts, too, heading for the women's restroom. I watch her wipe tears from her eyes en route.

My eyes narrow. "Why did you talk to her like that?"

Blake tosses a hand in the air. "I'm *sorry*."

"You sounded like a bully," I say.

He finally looks me in the eye. "I am so sorry, babe. Really, I am. It's just... I'm just really protective of Jamie, that's all. You *see* how he reacted."

"Yeah, well, those notes shook Melanie up too. What was she *supposed* to do with them?"

He nods earnestly. "You're right, you're right. I feel awful. I'll make it up to her, I promise. Please don't hate me for this, baby. It's just... it's like a reflex. When people I care about get hurt, I kinda... lash out. Just with my mouth, of course. I say things I don't mean. I've just been so worried about Jamie lately, and the way people have been judging us..."

I study his face. "I haven't noticed anyone judging you. It seems to me like everyone's gone out of their way to be kind."

"Oh, you mean like Natalie at the bonfire the other night?" he shoots back, riding a fresh wave of indignation.

"She was awful to *me*," I remind him. "And okay, maybe she said a couple of nasty things to Jamie too, but only because she's so hung up on you. But other than that..."

Blake laughs ruefully. "You have no idea what we've been through."

I lean in closer. "Then tell me."

He squeezes his eyes together, then peers at me intently. "It's been crazy. Jamie and I ... we've gotten death threats, hate mail ... you just don't get how evil people can be when they blame you for some horrible accident."

"I haven't heard the first word about anybody blaming you—"

"Then you haven't been living my life!"

His eyes melt when he sees me cower. "Oh, baby, I'm sorry! See, this is what I've been trying to shield you from. The people at our school—they're okay, most of them, anyway. But the people from *Cara's* school—they've been ruthless. Those notes Melanie got? Those are just one more twist of the knife. I don't think Jamie can take much more. That's why he's been so weird lately. That's why I reacted like such a maniac when Melanie told us about the notes. I don't want this terrible tragedy to end up ruining Jamie's life." He chokes up a little. "He's my best friend."

I reach out to touch his arm as Jamie and Melanie walk back to our booth, clinging shakily to each other's hands.

Blake jumps to his feet. "Melanie, I'm *so sorry*," he gushes. "I was totally out of line. You just ... you caught me off guard, that's all."

Everyone settles back into their seats, Jamie averting his eyes. Melanie clears her throat and smooths her hair.

"I was explaining to Anne—not that it excuses my behavior—but I was explaining how Jamie and I have gotten all kinds of nasty notes, phone calls, death threats—you name it—we've just been harassed to death since Cara died. It's the people at her school. I guess they just can't accept that she's gone, and Jamie and I are the ones who couldn't save her. I can take it; hell, I don't even *blame* the haters. They cared about Cara. I totally respect them for that."

He pauses, staring at his hands folded on the table. "Besides, they're not the only ones who blame me; god knows I blame myself. If only they knew they couldn't possibly beat me up as much as I beat up myself."

Jamie's glaring at him again.

"I had no idea," Melanie says. "I'm sorry. If I'd known..."

"*I'm* sorry," Blake repeats. "We didn't *want* you to know. I guess that's another reason I'm so upset...these assholes dragging you beautiful, innocent girls into this mess—"

"Cut it out, Blake," Jamie mutters curtly.

Blake shakes his head briskly. "What do you mean?"

Jamie glances at him. "I mean cool it. Shut the hell up." His voice is a chilling monotone.

Melanie and I gasp a little, as if all the oxygen has suddenly been sucked from the room. Jamie's words were so quiet, yet so...charged. I guess I have to take people's word for it that he used to idolize Blake. He clearly doesn't anymore.

Now Blake is glaring at *him*. But when he notices Melanie and me looking at him, his face softens. "You're right, bro," he tells Jamie in a conciliatory tone. "I don't want to pull these girls into this mess any more than you do. I just had to explain why I reacted the way I did. I won't bring it up again. This is *our* cross to bear...right?"

They exchange another charged glance, Jamie's expression dripping with contempt.

"So," Blake says, breaking the tension by clapping his hands together. "Change of subject."

We exchange anxious glances, but Melanie looks suddenly emboldened and sits up straight.

"Just one thing," she says.

Oh god...

"Yeah?" Blake says genially.

She ponders her thoughts for a moment, then says, "These notes are specifically about Jamie. Why would that be?"

"And then after the second note, Melanie thought we had to tell the guys, and that's when everything blew up, and—"

"Breathe, E, breathe," Sawyer tells me.

I called him as soon as Blake dropped me off, and I've never been so relieved to hear his voice. The voice of familiarity. The voice of sanity. The voice of simplicity. The voice of my blissfully uncomplicated past.

I insisted that Blake drop me off first after our date, telling him I didn't feel well. I was eager to escape the tension that never quite dissipated and wanted to avoid time alone with him. I'm not really sure why—yes, he was a jerk to Melanie, but he apologized, and he explained what he and Jamie have been going through. I had no idea about all that; I feel terrible for them, and I guess it adds context to the notes.

But I still can't shake my feeling of unease... the jarring

antagonism between Blake and Jamie, the ongoing angst of finding myself somehow embroiled in some poor girl's death, Blake's sudden flash of anger when Melanie mentioned the notes...I care about Blake, I really do. I might even be falling in love with him, like he said he's falling in love with me. Maybe that's why I can't loosen the knot in my stomach; maybe I'm scared of falling in love, so I'm looking for flaws. I don't know, I don't know, I don't know...

After I catch my breath, I finish getting Sawbones up to speed on the past few drama-filled days of my life. I tell him about Blake's reaction to the notes and his explanation, and then our mutual agreement that, even though we can't quite figure out why Jamie is being singled out, Natalie is the most likely culprit.

"Well," I qualify to Sawbones, "Blake and Melanie and I agree."

"Hmmm," he says. "So this Jamie guy doesn't think it's her?"

I shrug. "I dunno...he won't really say. Plus, people from Cara's school are apparently sending hate mail too, so I guess there are countless possibilities. But whenever we talk about it, Jamie just kinda sits there with his head hanging. It's all so upsetting to him."

"Why don't you and Blake ever hang out by yourselves?"

Okay, *that* was a total non sequitur. "What?"

"Don't get defensive; I'm just wondering why you two aren't ever really alone together."

"Jamie's his best friend," I say, trying to conceal the

edge in my voice. Why does Sawbones make me feel so self-conscious about my relationship with Blake?

"Yeah, they sound like they have barrels of fun together," Sawbones says. "Do you think maybe Blake is secretly gay?"

My jaw drops and I squeeze my eyes shut. "*What?*"

"Again, *don't get defensive*, but I can't help getting the feeling that he seems to be using you as some kind of...cover."

I search for words, then simply say in as non-defensive a tone as I can muster, "Blake is not gay."

"Mmmm," Sawbones says, clearly unconvinced. "It would explain a couple of things."

"Such as...?"

"The vibe you describe between Blake and Jamie...sexual tension, maybe? And it would explain why somebody is trying to warn your girlfriend to stay away from Jamie."

I'm too flabbergasted to speak. "That is...that is..."

"Logical?" Sawbones suggests.

I sputter a bit longer, then say, "Blake and I have had plenty of alone time."

Sawbones thinks about this, then asks, "You've had sex?"

"No!" I say. "God, what do you think of me? I've only known him a couple of weeks."

"Kind of my point..."

"*And yet*...and yet I'm very clear he's not gay. In fact, he's invited me to have Sunday dinner with his family tomorrow. *Without* his best friend, for the record."

Should I tell Sawbones that Blake is falling in love with me? Of course not. He'll just repeat my own words back to me: I've only known him a couple of weeks.

Still, I can tell that Blake's feelings are real. I can tell his kisses are real. Can't I?

I suddenly stun myself by feeling tears springing to my eyes. I hastily swallow the lump in my throat.

"E...?" Sawbones ventures warily.

I make some kind of mumbling sound.

"E, are you crying?"

I roll my eyes. "No, moron," I say, my voice a little stronger than before.

He pauses, then says, "Okay. Look, Ann-with-an-E: I've never so much as laid eyes on this guy. I don't have any answers, and I certainly don't want to hurt the feelings of the girl I adore more than any other person on earth. Just know I want the best for you. And know that the only reason I have questions and suspicions is because..."

"Is because why?"

"Is because *you* have questions and suspicions. Including, I'm guessing, the suspicion neither of us wants to say out loud."

My pulse quickens and I grip the phone tighter. "What?" I ask in a small voice.

He hesitates a beat, then says, "If Blake isn't gay, or for that matter, even if he is..."

"Yes...?"

"Then I'm wondering if there's more to the drowning story than we know."

"You can do it, sweetheart."

"Mom? Is that you?"

"Yep. Right here by your side."

I rub my eyes. "Why can't I see you?"

"Remember what Dr. Sennett said, sweetie: you don't have to see me to know I'm here."

"But why can't I see you?"

"You'll see me soon enough, when the time is right. Just not quite yet. Keep steering, honey."

"Oh, yeah, right. Wait a second ... whoa! Is this a plane I'm flying?"

"Yep. I turned it over to you."

"But I don't know how to fly!"

"Yes, you do. You just don't know that you do. You're doing great."

"Oh my god ... hold everything! This is ridiculous. I do not know how to fly!"

"Yes, you do. You just don't know that you do."

"You just said that. But I don't! Please ... don't say it again."

"Trust yourself, Anne. You know more than you think you do."

But I'm so freaked out that I decide the only thing to do is to fly the plane really low. The closer I am to the ground, the safer I feel. But this isn't working. I keep flying through tree limbs and bumping into buildings.

"You have to fly higher," Mom says.

"No! I have to be able to see the ground."

"Then you'll crash. Look at what you're doing; even though you're still in the air—barely—you're hitting everything in sight. What's safe about this?"

"It's safer than being too high! I'm scared of being too high."

"It doesn't work that way, honey. You were meant to fly higher than this. Being cautious is just going to cause you to crash."

"I don't care! I'm scared! I'm scared of going higher."

"Suit yourself. But this—this crazy ride—is the alternative to not increasing your altitude. This is the ride you have in store if you insist on holding back. You've got to let go, Anne. You have to rise to your potential."

"I'm too scared! What should I do, Mom? What should I do?"

"You should trust yourself."

I glimpse her from the corner of my eye, sitting in the co-pilot's seat. "Hey... Mom! You're here! I see you now!"

But when I turn for a better look, she's gone.

"Too late!" I say, crying and laughing at the same time. "I saw you! And surprise, I didn't freak out! I told you I could handle it. Oh, Mom... I saw you..."

My lashes flutter, then start to focus on my bedroom, illuminated by silky moonlight seeping through the blinds.

My heart is racing, but a smile is on my face.

I saw my mom... just for an instant, but I saw her. It felt so real. That plane ride was crazy, but even amid the chaos, her words were as clear as a bell:

You should trust yourself.

FIFTEEN

"And he told me if I ever made him sit in Santa's lap again, he'd kick him in the shins!"

Blake's family and I laugh at his mother's story, our silverware clinking against her good china.

"That's our Blake," his mother says cheerfully. "Even when he was three, he had a mind of his own." She glances at me, then adds, "But always such a *good* boy."

Blake exaggerates an *aw shucks* grin, and we laugh some more. He looks so cute, so boyish eating his mom's roast beef and listening to her stories. Most guys would cringe in a situation like this, but Blake seems to love it. He and his mom practically ooze adoration for each other. Garrett and his dad are clearly bit players in the dynamic. Garrett seems a little churlish, but his dad chuckles along gamely while occasionally adding a good-natured dig.

Blake really *is* light years more mature than most guys his age, winking at his mother rather than scowling at her, keeping the stories going rather than nipping them in the bud. I think this is why people sometimes react oddly to him. He's just so much more *together* than they expect him to be.

Right?

I impatiently shake Uncle Mark's words from my head: *almost too smooth.*

"What is it, dear?" Blake's mother asks me, and I feel my neck grow warm.

"What do you mean?" I ask.

"You looked preoccupied."

"Oh … no … just enjoying the story …"

His dad clears his throat. "Well, we've been regaled with Blake stories for an hour straight. Tell us about *you*, Anne."

"Well, I—"

"She's very smart," his wife tells him. "Brilliant, even, right, Anne?"

"Gosh, no …"

"Oh, she's just being modest," she tells her husband and sons, dismissing my denial with a wave of her hand. "Blake says she'll probably be the class valedictorian. And she's a reader, just like—"

She sucks in her breath abruptly and all eyes fall on her.

"It's okay to talk about her," Blake says softly. He turns toward me and squeezes my hand. "Cara was a big reader too."

"Oh …"

His mother looks at me intently. "I think the reason Blake cares so much for you is that you understand what he's going through. Your parents' accident—that's just so terrible, dear; I'm so sorry you have that cross to bear. But it gives depth and sensitivity that not many people your age can relate to. You know, even before Cara's accident, Blake was wise beyond his years. I'm guessing you were too. Add that to the fact that you've experienced tragedies so young in your life, and it just puts you on a whole different plane. I mean, how many other teenagers could possibly—"

"Any dessert, Mom?"

She casts Garrett an irritated glance. "I was talking," she tells him through gritted teeth.

"Sorry. I thought you were finished."

"I was in mid-sentence."

"Sue me," he mutters, eliciting an icy glare.

It occurs to me that Garrett acts a lot like Jamie does around Blake. And, duh...it makes a lot of sense. Blake's charisma tends to overshadow everything in the room, every*body* in the room. Sexual tension? Ridiculous. His own brother acts that way around him. People are just jealous of him, that's all. It's Occam's razor writ large: the simplest explanation is usually the right one. *Overanalyze much, Sawbones?*

Then again, Sawyer had a point: the only reason he had questions and suspicions is because *I* planted them. Being with Blake around his family has given me a lot of clarity. *I'm* the one who overthinks everything. I breathe a sigh of relief as I glean that Blake's and my relationship might actually be a lot less complicated than I feared, creepy anonymous notes notwithstanding. Even the notes are starting to seem less ominous. True, Blake overreacted, but once we got that tension out of the way, talking with the guys about the notes kind of demystified them. Worries aren't nearly as unsettling when you expose them to the light of day. I'm glad Melanie ignored my advice and went with her gut.

I'm feeling lighter on my feet by the minute.

———————

"And it was after he blew out his knee that we started playing golf together."

I dry a dish as Blake's dad hands it to me, enjoying this alone-time with him to get a father's perspective of a son who, according to his mother, is virtually perfection personified. His dad's stories are more prosaic, more understated—anecdotes indicating pride in his son in a measured, modest way.

I love seeing Blake through both sets of eyes. It was kind of the opposite for me: Mom kept me down to earth while Dad practically shouted my fabulosity from the rooftops. Mom was like a coach who saw my potential, Dad like a cheerleader who saw absolutely no room for improvement.

God, I miss them. Seeing the dynamic play out as a mirror image in another home—a home where I'm greeted with open arms, welcomed into the fold—is like being wrapped in a warm blanket. I could stand here at the sink with Blake's dad all day.

"Sorry that Blake's mom tends to go a little overboard," he tells me, handing me another plate. "Her protectiveness went into overdrive when he was diagnosed with cancer." He glances at me. "You'd heard about that, right?"

I nod. "Yes ... "

"Everything's fine now—well, mostly fine—but when she thought she might lose him, she became a real mother bear. What can I say? He's a little spoiled."

I shake my head. "No, no, I don't think so. I just think he knows how loved he is. That's a great thing."

Blake's dad offers a cryptic *mmmmmmm*, but then his face brightens. "I'll say one thing for him," he tells me. "He's got excellent taste in women."

I smile, drying the last dish as his dad drains the sink.

"Did you like Cara?" I ask him.

"Oh, yeah," he says, wiping his hands on a dishtowel. "Very sweet girl. The accident was ... devastating. She and Blake were very close—*too* close, really, for teenagers. Too close emotionally, I mean. I always thought they should be dating other people, not be exclusive at such a young age."

"I just think Blake's not into superficial relationships," I say. His dad nods but averts his eyes.

"Kids have all the time in the world for a committed relationship," he says, and I wonder if the irony strikes him. Cara didn't have all the time in the world. My parents didn't have all the time in the world. Nobody has all the time in the world. The clock's ticking for all of us, sometimes faster than we realize. Maybe it was a blessing for Cara to have so much love and commitment so early in life. Maybe it was a blessing for Blake, too, even though it intensified his grief. He's coping, right? He's moving on, even while honoring her memory. Bringing flowers to her mother every Sunday—what a touching gesture. I wonder when he does it.

Maybe he'll take them to her after he drops me off today. Speaking of which …

"Gee, I didn't realize it was so late," I say, glancing at the clock on the kitchen wall. "I've got a paper to finish. Better get going."

His dad offers a gallant bow from the waist, then takes my hand and kisses it. "It's been a pleasure, madam."

"Aaaaahhh, the pleasure has been all mine, kind sir," I say with a little curtsy.

I dry my hands on the dish towel, then walk down the hall into the great room.

"—*told* you, I will *not* let you be alone with—"

Garrett spots me in the doorway and blushes. Whatever he was telling Blake in a hushed tone when I walked in, I clearly wasn't meant to overhear.

"Anne … " he says.

Blake jumps up from the couch and walks over to my side. "We have a couple of bathrooms that need cleaning if you're still in the mood for chores," he says, kissing my cheek.

"The least I could do was help wash the dishes," I tell him, trying to match his breezy tone but still rattled by whatever Garrett was telling him when I walked in.

Garrett stares at the carpet.

"Um, I really should be going," I say. "I've got a paper due tomorrow, so … "

"Sure, sure," Blake says. "Ready, Garrett?"

I peer quizzically at Garrett. He's coming too?

"Yeah," he says, getting up from the recliner.

"I have to drop Garrett off at a friend's house after I take you home," Blake says.

Okay. Nothing weird about that, right? It's just that Garrett was in the car when Blake picked me up earlier, too. Of course, I thought nothing of it at the time. But his words ... the words I interrupted when I walked into the room ... are echoing in my head: *I will not let you be alone with—*

With who? Me? This is Blake's younger brother we're talking about. Why would that be his call?

And why the hell would he care?

SIXTEEN

"Did you finish your paper?"

I nod, taking the sandwich from the baggie in my brown paper bag. "I was up till midnight, but I cranked it out."

Blake and I are having lunch at a picnic table outside the cafeteria. I'd suggested privacy for a couple of reasons: Things seem to have smoothed over since I pissed off Lauren last week about the note, but I'm still wary of invading her space. Here I come, not only barging into her and Melanie's friendship but making a habit of arranging double dates with Mel, right on the heels of Lauren's breakup. I can only imagine how threatened she must feel. How would *I* have felt if some interloper had suddenly insinuated herself into my friendship with Sawbones, particularly if I'd been especially vulnerable at the time?

I get it, so I'm trying to back off a bit and give Lauren and Melanie a little space. I think everything's cool, but I don't want to screw anything up. Lauren and Melanie are the only girlfriends I have on Hollis Island. Maybe it's my imagination, but my other classmates seem to be keeping their distance. Is it because I've gotten so close to Blake so quickly? Do people resent it, like Natalie does? Do they think I'm a flake, or worse, an insensitive jerk? A full-of-myself diva? Do they mistrust me? Do they mistrust Blake?

Speaking of whom ...

I'd hoped Blake would volunteer information at lunch today about the conversation I interrupted at his house. I still can't shake Garrett's intensity about insisting he won't leave Blake alone with ... with whom? It *has* to be me. Who else could he have been talking about? But there has to be some easy explanation—the brothers were pretty much talking in shorthand, like there was some deal, some arrangement, that they'd both agreed to well before the conversation took place, like the way some siblings agree to take turns riding shotgun in the car or whatever. It's a brother thing, right? So why wouldn't Blake just tell me what they were talking about? He's got to know I'm curious.

But all Blake is doing is making small talk, munching an apple while I eat my sandwich in the warm muggy breeze. I can smell the salt in the air. How crazy that I used to count the days until our next beach visit. Now that I live here, I haven't been to the beach a single time. It's just a couple of blocks over, and yet it seems almost sacrilegious to go there without my parents. Maybe one day soon, I'll allow myself to revisit the girl I was before they died. Or maybe that girl died that day too. Maybe that's why I've gotten so close to Blake so fast; he's my express-train ticket to my new life.

"...Mr. Loring's class?"

I squint at Blake. "Sorry; what did you say?"

"I was asking about your test in Mr. Loring's class," Blake says, his tone a little peevish. "You seem awfully distracted."

I shake my head. "No, no...sorry. My brain's still a little fried from staying up late to finish my paper."

His expression clouds over. "And that's *my* fault?"

"What?" I peer at him closer. "What do you mean?"

"I mean if I hadn't invited you to dinner yesterday, you could have been home working on your precious paper. So sue me, for god's sake."

"No. No! That's not what I meant at all. I'm sorry, I had a great time at your house. *Really.* I was so happy to meet your parents. Please don't think that's what I meant..."

He sets his jaw and glowers into space.

Oh god. Can I do *anything* right these days?

"Blake, *please* don't be mad at me."

But he's still glaring straight ahead. I lean in and peck him on the cheek. "You're a total goofball if you think I'd rather do homework than hang out with you," I say in his ear.

He holds his pose for a moment, then his face softens. "You're sure?" he asks me.

"Uh, duh," I say, lightly squeezing a knuckle into his dimple, desperate to inject some levity into such a strange, fraught moment. How did things go south so quickly? How totally tone-deaf am I becoming to my interactions with other people? Have I turned into a self-absorbed twit since my parents died?

"Prove it," Blake says, but his voice is playful. "Go for a drive with me after school today."

I consider his words for a moment. A drive ... just the two of us? That would be a first. It actually sounds pretty awesome ...

I pop the side of my head with my hand. "Can't."

Uh-oh. The sullen expression is settling back into his face.

"I'm *sorry*," I say. "It's kind of annoying, but my aunt decided I should see a therapist for a few sessions, you know, to help deal with my parents' death. I just remembered I have an appointment after school."

I study his face to gauge his reaction, but for a long moment his expression is inscrutable.

"I'm really sorry," I say.

He finally shrugs. "It's okay. Really. I think it's a good idea you're seeing a therapist. People have told me I should do that too, but, I dunno, I just feel like I should be strong enough to deal with things myself. Plus, I just remembered, I'm volunteering at the children's hospital after school today."

I nod. "Maybe that's something we can do together after my counseling sessions are over. I'd love that."

He tosses his apple core into a trash can.

"Don't be mad?" I cajole.

He's silent for a moment, then sticks his tongue out at me. I laugh at him.

"I can never stay mad at you," he tells me, then kisses me on the lips. "Gotta go. I've got my own test to study for."

As he walks away, I wave to him and call, "Good luck at the children's hospital."

It's after Blake is out of earshot that I hear a voice behind me say, "Please."

I turn toward the voice and see a guy at the next picnic table over. He looks familiar from a couple of my classes, but I don't know his name.

I look at him quizzically, not sure if he's talking to me.

"What did you say?" I ask him.

"The *children's hospital*?" the guys says, his voice dripping with sarcasm.

"Blake volunteers there," I say.

"Right. Whatever you say."

My brow furrows. "What are you insinuating?"

The guy presents his palms as peace offerings. "Nothing, nothing. I'm sure that's exactly how Blake spends his time. I'm guessing a story will be circulating by next week that he's donated a kidney to one of the tots."

My jaw drops subtly as I try to wrap my head around his words.

"Are you saying he's lying?"

"*Nah*," the guy insists disingenuously. "Lying would be a flaw. No chance of that." He gets up from the bench, grabs his backpack, and brushes past me. "Helluva guy, that Blake," he murmurs. "A legend in his own mind."

A breeze buffets my cheek as he walks away. I squeeze my arms together, suddenly chilled.

What the hell was *that* all about?

"So you had fun yesterday?"

I nod as Aunt Meg drives me to my second appointment with Dr. Sennett. "Yeah. His family's great."

I twist my fingers together in my lap. I'm still tossing around in my mind what happened at lunch. Everything seemed so strange: Blake's sudden sullenness, that guy's random insinuations... Why can't I seem to go more than an hour without utter confusion clouding my brain?

"Honey?"

I look at Aunt Meg. "Mmmm-hmmmm?"

"Honey, this is probably nothing, but... "

My eyebrows knit together. "Yes?"

Aunt Meg pauses, seemingly bouncing words around in her head.

"What is it?" I prod.

She touches her bottom lip with her index finger. "Probably nothing, like I said. But... remember when Blake told us that he brings flowers every week to the mother of the girl who died?"

My stomach muscles clench ever so slightly. "Yeah?"

She glances at me, then refocuses on the road. "You know I told you that I work with the girl's aunt? Cathleen Wexler?"

"Yeah...?"

Aunt Meg takes a deep breath, then continues: "Honey, Cathleen told me that Blake has never brought Cara's mother flowers. She said the family hasn't seen or heard from him since

Cara's memorial service. Not that there's anything necessarily wrong with that, but—"

"Why would you talk to your co-worker about our private conversations at the dinner table?" I say, my voice tighter than I intended.

Aunt Meg looks a little flummoxed, but then she casts me a sharp look. "Why *wouldn't* I? I was just making conversation. Here's a guy that we mutually know, and he's been to my house for dinner, so..."

"*Still.*"

Aunt Meg stops at a red light, then takes a right, gripping the steering wheel with both hands, looking intently ahead.

"I'm sorry," I finally say, touching my fingers against my mouth. "I didn't mean to snap at you. I just..."

I just have a brand-spanking-new reason to feel a new knot in my stomach. *Quit blaming Aunt Meg for your own insecurities, idiot.*

"I'm not even sure why I'm bringing it up," Aunt Meg says, her voice gentle again.

"Isn't it a good possibility that your coworker just doesn't *know* about the flowers?" I ask, trying to sound as nonchalant as possible.

Aunt Meg shakes her head reluctantly. "Cathleen and her sister are really close. Cara's mother is actually the one who brought up Blake in a recent conversation. She was wondering how he's doing, since she hasn't seen him or heard from him since... well, you know."

My mind bounces around a couple of alternate possible explanations: Maybe Cara's dad meets Blake at the door, then declines to give the flowers to his wife for fear of upsetting her? Maybe Blake leaves the flowers at Cara's gravesite, assuming her mother will collect them? But I stay silent. I don't know what to think. I'm just so tired of feeling defensive any time Blake's name comes up.

"It's not a big deal that he doesn't bring her flowers," Aunt Meg clarifies, which serves only to tighten the knot in my stomach, "but it's just so strange he'd volunteer information that isn't true. It's not like anybody asked him about it."

"You *did* ask him about Cara," I say, and god, now I not only sound defensive, I sound like a petulant kid. "You're the one who brought her up at dinner."

"I certainly didn't ask him about bringing flowers to her mother," Aunt Meg says.

"Well, maybe he felt like he was on the spot."

"Exactly," she says, nodding too eagerly. "I really think that explains it. I just... thought I should tell you."

A heavy silence hangs in the air.

"Anne?"

"Yep," I murmur, staring straight out the passenger window.

"Maybe you should talk to Dr. Sennett about Blake."

"I saw my mom in my dream."

Dr. Sennett's eyebrows arch.

"Just for a second," I qualify. "We were communicating, though. She was trying to get me to fly a plane. Actually, she was insisting that I fly it. I kept telling her I didn't know how—I was so scared, so I was flying really low, knocking into trees and buildings—but she told me I *did* know how, I just didn't know I knew."

I scan Dr. Sennett's face for her reaction. "Is it torture to have to listen to people's dreams for an hour?" I ask tentatively.

She laughs. "Nothing's torturous about spending time with you, Anne," she says. "You're a delightful, insightful young woman."

"Mmmmmm. Actually, I'm a mess."

Dr. Sennett leans closer. "How so?"

I peer out her window. "The guy I told you about last week? The guy I'm dating? I keep getting these weird vibes."

"Go on..."

I shrug. "I can hardly even think of any examples," I say, averting my eyes as a dozen or so examples pop effortlessly into my brain. I just can't stand the thought of articulating them. My head hurts from thinking so much.

"What does your gut tell you?" Dr. Sennett says.

I smile ruefully. "My gut is seriously confused. I'm all over the map. One minute, I'm jumping for joy that I've found the greatest guy in the world. The next minute, I feel like I don't know him at all."

I pause, then say, "He kinda snapped at my girlfriend the other night—no biggie, just this quick flash of temper that really caught me off guard—and I thought, 'Whoa, I didn't see *that* coming.' But even saying this out loud makes me feel silly, like, 'Flash of temper: alert the media!' Am I just *looking* for flaws?"

Dr. Sennett taps her pencil against the arm of her chair. "You didn't go looking for that."

"Yeah, but how ridiculous are my standards if I can't even tolerate a little snippiness?"

"Initially, you called it a flash of temper."

I roll my eyes dismissively. "Does it matter what I call it?"

She ponders the question, then says, "I think it does."

My eyes fall. "I want this to be right."

Dr. Sennett adjusts her glasses. *"Wanting* it to be right doesn't mean it is."

I squeeze my hands together. "I really think I'm overreacting." *And that whole lying-about-the-flowers thing? I'll just keep that pesky example to myself. Not even worthy of a mention.*

Dr. Sennett leans onto her forearms. "Let's get hypothetical for a minute: You've decided it's *not* right. For whatever reason, you decide this guy is not for you. Poof, just like that, one day he's in your life, the next day, he's gone. Where does that leave you?"

I bite my lip to steady my suddenly trembling chin. "Alone," I say, in barely a whisper.

"Alone, huh," Dr. Sennett muses. "Let's see: You have your aunt and uncle. You have whatever girlfriend Mr. Wonderful snapped at. You have me. You have teachers who care about you, friends back home, other relatives ... And most importantly, you have a *future*. A huge, unlimited future that will bring a whole new slew of people into your life, people you can't even imagine right now. But can you try anyway? Can you use your imagination and try to picture your future?"

My eyes grow moist, blurring the trees outside Dr. Sennett's window. "I can't see Mom and Dad in my future. That's all I can picture: the things that are missing."

A long moment passes.

"Yet you'll march into your future anyway," Dr. Sennett finally says. "Even if you do nothing. Even if you tell yourself that whatever you're holding in your hands right now is all you can count on so you can't possibly let it go. You can't hold on tight enough to make time stand still, Anne. Your future is coming, whether you like it or not."

I sniffle and wipe a tear from my cheek.

"But you know what?" Dr. Sennett says in barely a whisper. "I think you're gonna like it just fine."

"You take it."

"No, *you* take it."

"No, you!"

Uncle Mark and I laugh at each other as we each reach for the last apple in the bowl, both of us passing through the kitchen from separate areas of the house before bedtime.

"I don't even like apples," Uncle Mark says. "Blechhhht."

I raise an eyebrow and point an index finger into the air. I retrieve a knife, cut the apple in half, and hand him his piece. His eyes sparkle as we dig into our halves.

He chews, then says with a full mouth, "You are brilliant."

I giggle. "That's what Blake's mom called me at dinner

yesterday. She was like, 'Aren't you brilliant or something?' And I was like, '*Duh*.'"

"Brilliance is hereditary, you know," Uncle Mark says, swallowing his bite. "Hey, speaking of brilliant, this indie movie that got awesome reviews at Sundance is playing at the university theater. Wanna go?"

I scrunch my eyebrows. "It's almost midnight."

"Yeah, I meant tonight," he deadpans, and I laugh at myself, squeezing my eyes shut.

"It'll be there all week, silly," he says. "Maybe over the weekend?"

"Hmmmmmm. Will you supply the apples?"

"Maybe *half* of one."

I nod sharply. "It's a date."

Uncle Mark tousles my hair. "You look just like your dad, you know."

I feel my face brighten. "People have always told me I look like Mom."

"No, you definitely inherited both your looks and your brilliance from my side of the family."

I laugh some more, loving Uncle Mark for being irreverent about my parents. Maybe we're finally moving past the pro-scribed discussions guided by the invisible hand of an expert.

We stand there a minute on the cool tile, then he says, "So, that psychiatrist lady ... that's going okay?"

"She's actually a psychologist," I say. "Yeah, it's going fine. She's really cool."

"Because you don't have to go if you don't want to, you know," Uncle Mark says.

"Aunt Meg actually forced me at gunpoint."

"Well, that's where I draw the line."

I wrinkle my nose at him playfully. "It really was thoughtful of Aunt Meg to set it up. Okay, initially I thought, 'That Aunt Meg is quite the control freak'"—I say this in an exaggerated, sing-song voice—"but it does help to have someone to talk things over with."

Uncle Mark puts an arm around my shoulder and squeezes me tightly. "You know you can always talk things over with me, sweetie...right?"

I'm so touched that I'm momentarily speechless.

"I'll always be here for you, Annie."

I swallow a lump in my throat as he folds me into a big hug.

SEVENTEEN

"Hand it over!"

I gasp and run over to Melanie's locker. I've just gotten to school, and I have to pass her locker to get to mine.

But it's not Melanie standing at her locker. It's Blake. Blake and Natalie. She's standing there seemingly frozen in space, her eyes as wide as saucers.

"You heard me," he tells her in a menacing growl, leaning so close to her face that their noses are almost touching.

Melanie, who's just arrived at school herself, rushes to my side. "What is going *on*?" she asks in a frantic whisper.

"Now!" Blake bellows to Natalie as an ever-growing curious crowd collects.

"You … you don't understand," she says plaintively.

Lauren rushes up to Melanie and me, muttering, "What the hell?"

Blake is still hulking over Natalie, who looks like she might actually implode with fear. I rush to the locker and step between the two of them, locking eyes with Blake. His are bulging with rage.

"What's going on?" I ask in the calmest voice I can muster.

"I caught our little note-writer red-handed," he says, his eyes once again boring into Natalie's.

"No!" she protests weakly.

"Hand. Me. The note," he says chillingly.

Enough of a crowd has gathered that an adult is finally in the mix. Mr. Loring, my calculus teacher, rushes up to us. He looks almost comically harmless in his short-sleeve dress shirt and bow-tie, but I'm ridiculously glad to see him.

"What's going on?" he asks Blake.

Blake's eyes scan the crowd: Natalie, me, Melanie, Lauren ... He seems conflicted for a nanosecond but quickly recovers and puffs out his chest.

"Natalie just put a note in my friend's locker," he tells Mr. Loring.

"And why is that your concern?"

Again, a wave of ambivalence washes over Blake's face, but only for a moment. "Someone's been passing anonymous notes to her. Notes about my friend. So I've scoped out her locker for the past couple of days to see if I could catch the person in the act."

Blake presents his hand, as if he's serving up Natalie on a platter. She turns almost literally green.

"And *whose* locker is it?" Mr. Loring says.

"Mine," Melanie says, stepping forward. "Blake is right,

Mr. Loring. Someone's been sending me anonymous notes. They're no big deal—just immature kid stuff—but I told Blake about them over the weekend, so I guess he was watching out for me. We don't know for sure, but we think Natalie might be the one writing the notes."

She glares at Natalie, who wilts before our eyes.

Mr. Loring turns toward her. "You've been putting notes in her locker?"

Natalie trembles. "Just two. But they're not from me."

"And who might they be from?" he persists.

Natalie's chin trembles. "I promised I wouldn't tell."

Mr. Loring purses his lips. "Let's take this to the office."

"Mr. Loring," Blake says, his voice now measured and reasonable, "I think we can settle this among ourselves, if you don't mind. Now that we know who's been planting the notes, I don't think we'll have to worry about this anymore."

"What a stand-up guy," Lauren mutters under her breath.

Blake is giving Natalie a studied stare, his expression a mixture of condescension and contempt.

"Are there any threats in the notes?" Mr. Loring asks.

Natalie's face crinkles like a leaf. "I don't even know! I haven't even read the stupid things!"

"No threats," Blake interjects quickly. "She's got a crush on me and is trying to stir things up with my buddy and his girlfriend."

Natalie squeezes her eyes shut.

Mr. Loring looks at Melanie. "No threats?"

"No, sir," she assures him earnestly. "No threats."

Then Melanie tosses a haughty look at Natalie and adds, "I'm not afraid of her."

Mr. Loring hesitates a moment, then tells Melanie, "Open your locker and show me the note, please."

Melanie, Lauren, and I exchange glances. Jamie's nowhere in sight, but we know he'd be mortified to have half the school watch the saga unfold.

"I really think we can handle this ourselves..." Melanie says.

"The note, please," Mr. Loring says curtly.

Melanie sighs and opens her locker, plucking a sealed blank envelope from the top. She swallows hard, then hands it to Mr. Loring.

He glances hastily around the hallway. "Everyone else, please resume what you were doing," he says.

The crowd starts reluctantly dispersing, everyone except Blake, Natalie, Melanie, Lauren, and me.

"Girls?" Mr. Loring says to Lauren and me. The two of us drop our chins and start slinking down the hall, trying to walk slowly enough to overhear what's going on.

But we have to keep moving, and soon we're out of earshot. Mr. Loring murmurs a few words we can't make out, then walks to his classroom. Lauren and I rush back to Mel's locker.

"I swear, I didn't write it!" Natalie is telling Blake and Melanie, now heaving full-fledged sobs.

"Where's the note?" I ask Blake.

He nods toward Mr. Loring's classroom. "He took it."

"What did it say?" Lauren asks breathlessly.

Natalie blurts out the answer. "It said, 'Why won't you listen to me?' That's all it said; that's it! And *I* didn't know what it said until Mr. Loring opened it!"

"Then why did you plant it in my locker?" Melanie asks.

"I didn't *plant* it," Natalie says through jagged sobs. "I *put* it in there. As a favor to a friend. I didn't know what the notes said; I didn't know they were freaking you out."

"Bullshit!" Blake says.

"It's true! I swear it's true!" she cries.

"Then who wrote the notes?" Melanie demands. "Who are you covering for?"

Natalie drops her head and shakes it. "I promised her I wouldn't tell. But I'll ask her today if it's okay. I'll tell her this has all blown up and become a huge mess. I promise, I'll ask her if I can tell, and if it's okay with her, I'll—"

"Why in the world," Lauren asks, "would you try to protect the privacy of a sniveling coward who goes around writing anonymous notes?"

"She's only trying to help," Natalie says, her eyebrows an inverted V over tear-stained eyes. "If you knew who it was, you'd understand. She isn't trying to freak anybody out. She's only trying to help."

We cast anxious glances at each other, which makes Natalie dissolve into a fresh round of tears. "I promise, I'll ask her today if I can tell you. I promise!"

Then she turns and runs down the hall, her shoes tap-tap-tapping against the linoleum as she buries her face in her hands.

As we watch her disappear into the crowd, Blake's eyes

narrow. "She's never been anything but a pain in my ass," he says, his voice hard and gravelly. "A goddamn pain in my ass."

"She's gone," Lauren says.

My eyes dart from her face to Melanie's and back again as I approach them at the lunch table. "What do you mean?" I ask.

"I mean Natalie wasn't in our second-period class," she says. "Word is she hightailed it out of school as soon as she was caught planting the note this morning."

I put my tray on the table and take my seat, though I know I won't be able to choke down even a bite.

"Has Jamie heard?" I ask. "I haven't seen him at all today."

Melanie sighs. "Poor Jamie. I've cornered him at least three times and he won't even talk about it. He just shakes his head and says, 'Whatever, just drop it, there's nothing to say.'" She snorts. "Tell that to the rest of the school. It's all anybody else is talking about. I guess you were right, Anne. Tell a couple of people, and before long the whole school's talking about it."

"It didn't help that Blake made a scene at the locker," I mutter, picking up a limp fry and then dropping it back onto the tray.

"What was he *supposed* to do?" Melanie asks. "He caught her red-handed!"

"I dunno," I say. "He just goes a little ... ballistic sometimes. If he'd been a little more discreet—if he'd been the *slightest* bit discreet—we could have wrapped all of this up privately and moved on. And why was he staking out your locker anyway, Mel? Did you even ask him to?"

She thinks about it, then waves a hand impatiently. "No, but I'm glad he did. It was a good idea; I guess it was just a matter of time before another note turned up."

"Maybe..." I murmur.

Lauren looks at me quizzically. "Why are you hating on Blake all of a sudden? God knows he annoys the hell out of *me*—so darn earnest—but aren't you glad he got to the bottom of this?"

"Uh," Melanie interjects, "considering *I'm* the one who was getting the notes, I think I'm the only one qualified to answer that question. Yes, I'm doing the happy dance that the mystery is solved."

I drum my fingers on the tabletop. "Except that it isn't," I say, more to myself than the others.

They lean in closer.

"What do you mean?" Melanie asks.

I pause, then shrug. "It still doesn't make any sense. Why would Natalie want to break up you and Jamie? And why did she react so strangely at the locker? She really *did* act clueless about what the notes said. And who's this other girl she's talking about?"

"You mean the fantasy girl who doesn't exist?" Melanie says.

"Why would that be so far-fetched?" I ask. "Blake says he and Jamie have been getting hate mail from people at Cara's school."

138

Mel shakes her head briskly. "Natalie has established herself as a lunatic. What did you expect her to do, admit it? I don't get why you think it would be so shocking for her to lie."

I stare blankly into space. "I just wouldn't expect her to lie so *well*..."

Lauren looks at us haltingly, opening her mouth to speak, then abruptly shutting it again.

"What?" Melanie asks her.

She bites her lip. "Well... there *is* one theory floating around, but it's really off the wall..."

Melanie makes a rolling motion with her hand.

Lauren shakes her head. "Let's just eat."

Melanie raises an eyebrow. "Uh, I don't think so. Spill it."

Lauren picks at her food some more. "I just hate fueling the stupid gossip," she says.

I lean into the table. "What did you hear?"

Lauren pauses a moment, then rolls her eyes in resignation. "Okay, fine. This is really screwy, but, whatever. Here goes: the thing I've heard a couple of people mention—even before the whole school found out about the notes—and these are people who don't even *know* the dead girl, mind you, so consider the source..." Lauren blows her bangs out of her face. "They're kinda floating the theory that maybe the dead girl isn't really... you know... technically dead."

Mel and I crinkle our brows.

"I've got to admit," Lauren continues, "it's the first thing that popped into my head when Natalie started yammering about some mystery girl, some girl whose identity she couldn't disclose for some unmentionable reason..."

"That's crazy," Melanie says. "Cara drowned that night."

Lauren gives us a steady gaze. "So say Blake and Jamie. But the body was never recovered. And the people I heard talking—they're friends with some kids at Cara's school—they said that apparently no one at the bonfire that night ever saw Cara go into the water. They say it would have been weird for her to go swimming at night, all by herself, and that most of them weren't even wearing bathing suits."

"What's weird about taking a swim on a beach in the middle of summer?" Melanie says. "And I thought *everybody* saw her go into the water. Or maybe I just assumed they did...?"

Lauren shakes her head. "They said that Blake and Cara went off alone... that they walked far enough down the beach that nobody else could see them... and then Blake came back to the bonfire alone. He pulled Jamie aside and the two of them took off in the direction he'd just come from. Nobody thought anything of it at the time; Blake didn't tell them what was up. Later, they heard Blake telling the police that Cara had gone for a swim and when he got worried she'd been gone too long, he went back and got Jamie so they could ride out on the jet ski and look for her. It was only after Blake and Jamie came back from the jet ski that anybody else at the bonfire even knew Cara was missing. Otherwise, they'd *all* have been looking for her. That was when somebody called 911."

"This is crazy," I say. "Why would they lie about Cara going swimming?"

"Why would *Blake* lie," Melanie corrects me delicately, then glances at me for a quick sensitivity check.

"So why would *Blake* lie?" I ask more petulantly than I intended. "And if she didn't drown that night, then where the hell is she and what the hell is she doing?"

"Sending notes to Melanie...?" Lauren ventures cautiously, but then shakes her head briskly. "This is obviously crazy talk. I told you, it was just a couple of stupid rumors I overheard, and from people who didn't even know Cara, mind you. Friends of friends, or in this case, acquaintances of acquaintances. You know how reliable *that* kind of information can be."

Melanie's eyebrows furrow. "Is there supposed to be some reason that Cara would have wanted to disappear?"

"Again," Lauren says, "I've just heard rumors, but, you know... the typical reason a girl her age would want to disappear."

We consider the implication, then Melanie gasps and fills in the blank:

"*Pregnant.*"

I feel my pulse quicken and instinctively press my parents' rings against my chest.

"Oh god, Anne... are you okay?" Melanie says, studying my face as if I'm a mutant lab specimen. "You look like you're about to hyperventilate."

"I'm fine," I snap, but I'm still breathing fast... *really* fast.

"Oh, Anne, we're just repeating stupid rumors," Melanie says, leaning closer and squeezing my arm protectively.

"Everybody knows how crazy Blake is about you; you can see it all over his face. We're just being silly and melodramatic."

"Right," Lauren says, nodding firmly. "Look, I'm so sorry I repeated those rumors. Anne, forget I said anything. I don't know what I was thinking. It's ridiculous to—"

I breathe out through an O in my mouth. "I need some air..."

"We'll come with you..."

"No, I'm good."

I jump out of my seat and head out of the cafeteria with my head tucked almost into my chest, my untouched tray of food still at the table.

"Anne? Are you okay?"

I glance up at Garrett just as I reach the hall, my head still spinning.

"Oh, hi..."

"Do you need to sit down?" he asks me, then takes my arm and starts guiding me back into the cafeteria.

I gently shake free. "I'm fine, really. I just need some air. I feel a little lightheaded..."

Blake walks up just as I'm about to bolt again.

"Are you okay?" he asks me anxiously.

"She's feeling lightheaded," Garrett tells him.

"Get her a chair," Blake says, but I shake my head, cringing amid all the attention.

"I'm fine, I'm fine," I tell them. "Really. I'm much better now. It was just a passing thing."

"It's those stupid notes," Blake fumes, but I shake my head again.

"I'm *fine*. I didn't have much of an appetite at lunch, so I didn't really eat anything, and I think I stood up too quickly..."

"Can I get you some water?" Garrett asks.

"No. Really. I'm okay. I just... I've got to get to class early so I can get some studying done. You guys go enjoy your lunch."

Garrett gauges Blake's reaction, then says, "If you're sure..."

I nod briskly, then manage a weak smile. "Thanks, though."

"Sure," Garrett says. "Well... take care of yourself, okay?"

He starts walking into the cafeteria, then turns back when Blake doesn't join him.

"You go on ahead," Blake tells him, still glued to my side. "And hey, I've got a yearbook meeting after school, so tell Mom I'll be home late."

Garrett pauses, then nods warily and walks inside.

"Baby, I can't stand to see you so upset," Blake coos, pressing me into a hug.

"I'm okay, really," I say, trying to extricate myself as discreetly as possible. "I just need a little air, a little space..."

"Baby, you and I need some time to get away from all this insanity and clear our heads. Let me take you to the beach after school."

My eyes narrow. "I thought you had a yearbook meeting."

"I just need to be alone with you," he says, caressing my cheek. "Please? Just the two of us?"

I hesitate.

"There *are* a few things I'd like to ask you about," I tell him, my voice slightly trembling.

"Of course," he says, leaning into my face. "You can ask me anything. I know the rumors have been flying since I made a scene at the locker. That was so stupid of me. I'm so sorry, babe; I just couldn't hide my anger when I caught Natalie red-handed. Knowing how much those notes upset you and Jamie...I just blew my top. Genius move, right? I couldn't have gotten tongues wagging any more if I'd shown up to school in the buff. I'm sorry."

I study his face for a moment, then ask, "Do you have any idea what other girl Natalie might have been talking about this morning? I really got the feeling there was more to the story than..."

"Natalie is full of crap," he says. "She's been obsessed with me since middle school. This is just her latest strategy for glomming onto my life. Plus, I heard she took off right after getting caught planting the note. She was loving the drama as long as she could skulk behind the scenes to do her dirty work. Once everything was out in the open, she turned tail like a sniveling coward."

I cringe a little. I don't know why it bothers me to hear Blake talk so harshly about Natalie; he certainly has every reason to be bitter. But she's so clearly fragile that his anger seems outsized, disproportionate, almost cruel, like swatting at a moth that doesn't have enough sense to give you a wider berth.

"Did Natalie know Cara?" I ask.

He shrugs. "I think they met once or twice. She's always trying to run in the same circles as me. I think she managed to crash a couple of parties. But Natalie was *nothing* to Cara, just like she's nothing to me."

Blake catches my eye, then leans in closer.

"I'm sorry, baby ... did I upset you?"

I shrug. "Natalie only has as much power as you give her. The fact that she gets such a rise out of you ... it just seems like a waste of energy and kinda ... mean, you know? It's like I told Melanie: Natalie's insecure, not vicious."

He runs his fingers through my hair. "I don't ever want you to think I'm mean, baby," he says, lowering his head until his eyes are level with mine. "It's just ... the way she talked to you that night at the bonfire, then the stupid notes. That's not okay."

I nod. "I know, I know ... It's just hard not to feel a little sorry for her."

"It's not hard for me. But you know what? I'm not wasting another second thinking or talking about that girl. After what happened this morning, I've got a strong feeling she'll be a non-issue from now on. But even if she writes a goddamn unauthorized biography about me, I'll just take a cleansing breath and let it roll right off my back. Just for you."

He flicks his index finger across my nose, and I smile.

"Hey, if I'm taking that kind of a bullet for you, I'll need a bigger smile than that," he says playfully, and I force a wider smile.

He leans in and kisses me.

"We'll drive to the beach right after school," he says. "We'll get away from all this craziness and have a chance to catch our breath. And you know you can ask me anything. Anything you like."

My eyes flicker in his direction. "You're okay with going to the beach?" I ask gingerly.

He ponders my question, then sets his jaw stoically. "I can't stay away from the beach for the rest of my life," he says. "And I know I can handle anything with you by my side."

I hesitate, then nod, averting my eyes. "I've really got to get to class..."

But Blake takes my arm as I begin walking away. "Anne?"

I glance at him. "Yeah?"

"I love you."

EIGHTEEN

"This is where it happened."

A sea breeze wafts through our hair as Blake and I stand at the shore, distant thunder churning in a slate-gray sky and waves nipping at our bare feet. We've walked silently on the sand for about three-quarters of a mile, but now that we've approached a rocky outcrop of the beach, Blake has stopped abruptly.

"Right here," he repeats in barely a whisper, peering out into the ocean and swallowing hard.

I reach for his hand and our fingers enfold. "Is this the first time you've been back since ... "

He nods, and I squeeze his hand harder.

"It was so *senseless*," he says, his deep blue eyes sad and angry at the same time.

A smattering of other people dot the shore, and we've passed a couple of swimmers, but I feel oddly secluded, as if the weight of the tragedy is closing in on us like a fog. As jolting as this day has been, this particular moment seems disembodied... gauzy and disconnected, with everything around us dissolving except for doleful stirrings from the sea. God... a poor girl *died* in that sea just a few short months ago, stupid rumors notwithstanding, and seeing Blake's expression now, I don't doubt that's exactly what happened. I've stood a dozen times or more on the roadside where Mom and Dad took their last breaths, and I'm all too familiar with the disbelieving look in Blake's eyes, the quickened breaths emanating from somebody whose body otherwise seems petrified, encased in grief.

Yes, I know the look. The way that Blake is staring into the ocean is the way I've stared at the asphalt where the drunk driver ran the stop sign and T-boned my parents' car. I've felt like if I stared hard enough, or long enough, I could make sense of the fact that my parents could be perfectly healthy one minute, dead the next, just as Cara was. It can't be that easy for life to be snuffed away, can it? Shouldn't the process of death be more mindful, more deliberate?

But destiny can't deliberate, and as much as I wish otherwise, destiny didn't give me the opportunity to intervene the night my parents were killed. It must be even harder for Blake. He *tried* to intervene, yet failed. He and Jamie. They had a chance to rescue Cara, the briefest window to change the course of history, to save a life. No wonder they're so wounded, so captive to the pain that binds and repels them simultaneously.

The waves are skittering up to the silver-speckled rocks. When high tide hits an hour from now, the water will pummel the rocks, smashing against them and leaving frothy spittle behind. Most of the rocks are jagged and uneven, but one is smooth and flat enough to sit on. I gently pull Blake toward it.

"Let's talk a minute ... okay?"

He nods and follows me to the rock. We sit in silence a few moments, still staring at the sea. A couple of raindrops skim our noses, the kind of raindrops that could be either a fleeting annoyance or the opening salvo of a pelting storm. I shiver even though the air is warm and muggy.

I inhale deeply, then say, "I know it's hard for you to be here, Blake, but I heard a few things today that kinda spooked me."

Another raindrop flecks my upper arm.

"That's why we're here, baby. I told you: you can ask me anything."

I nod and stare at my hands. "I don't want to upset you, but ... can you tell me what happened that night?"

My hands clench as I wonder anxiously whether I should disclose what I already know, or at least what I *think* I know. Is it some kind of betrayal that I've googled the accident, that I've collected bits and pieces of information here and there? Or is that a no-brainer, something anyone else in my position would do? I don't know; I just don't ever want Blake to think I'm sketchy. The way people are reacting to me these days, I barely trust myself to utter a word about *anything*. But even as I'm deliberating, I can tell he's collecting his thoughts. I stay quiet and wait for his response.

He takes a deep breath and rubs the back of his neck. "A few of us decided to have a little party on the beach," he says, his gaze still fixed on the ocean. "It wasn't even a party ... just a get-together with a few of Cara's friends. My friends could come too, of course, but these were mostly people from her school ... everyone except Jamie and me."

A seagull squawks nearby, skimming the surface of the water.

"Cara and I got to the party around nine that night. I think we were the last ones to get there," Blake continues. "Somebody had already built a bonfire, and people were roasting marshmallows, playing guitars, throwing Frisbees ... "

"Were they drinking?" I ask hesitantly "Were *you?*"

His eyes turn flinty for a nanosecond, but then they soften again. "I *never* drink," he says firmly. "When you survive cancer, you never take anything for granted again, and you'll be damned before you'll voluntarily screw up your own health. I'm sure other people in the group were drinking, but—"

"Was Cara?" I interject.

"No," he says. "She didn't drink either, and she definitely wouldn't drink on a date with me. I take my responsibilities very seriously when I'm with a girl. I take good care of myself and I take good care of the people I'm with."

I tighten my lips, wondering if the irony is striking him, but he seems unfazed. I'm also a little put off by his machismo, but he's probably just trying to impress me ... right? This is something every dad would like to hear when his daughter goes on a date, I guess. Blake seems very smooth about those kinds of things.

Uncle Mark's words echo in my ear—*almost too smooth*—

but I shake them impatiently from my thoughts. I'm clearly overthinking again.

"So, yeah, I guess some people were drinking, and somebody probably passed around a joint or two at some point, but nobody was wasted or anything. Cara and I were totally sober."

"Were any of them swimming?" I ask haltingly.

"Swimming? No. Well, yeah ... of course. I mean, we were at the *beach* in the middle of June, for crying out loud. Every once in a while, somebody would jump in and take a swim."

"And that's what Cara decided to do?"

"Yeah."

I detect the slightest edge in his voice. Am I going too far, asking too many questions? Is this even any of my business?

"I told you, Anne, you can ask me anything," he says, softening his tone as if he's reading my thoughts. "Yes, she decided to go for a swim. Yes, I beat myself up every day for letting her do it."

Letting her do it. My stomach clenches a bit.

"But what was the big deal?" he muses, more to himself than to me. "You're at the beach, you jump in for a quick swim ... "

"So you guys were all sitting around, then she ... "

"Um, Cara and I had actually gone off alone to take a walk," he says, "just the two of us. We'd been hanging with the group all night and wanted a few minutes alone. We walked for a while, then she said, you know, she wanted to cool off, jump in the water, take a little swim ... "

"So she was wearing her bathing suit?"

Again, his eyes turn flinty. "No, Anne, she was wearing a parka," he snaps. "I mean, it was *June*, after all."

I feel my cheeks turn warm, and he reaches abruptly for my hand. I instinctively pull it away, but then I reluctantly let him take it.

"I'm sorry, baby. Geez, why do I sound like such a jerk sometimes? It's just... the guilt does such a number on me." He takes another deep breath. "She had her bathing suit on under her shorts and T-shirt. She asked me to hold her clothes."

I nod, and he continues. "We were right here, right around these rocks, and I waited on the beach while she took a swim. The surf was rough—I didn't know *how* rough until later. The water looked calm enough, but apparently there was a strong undertow. I didn't know that... but even if I had, I don't think I would've really been concerned. She was a good swimmer— we'd been swimming in undertows our whole lives—and besides, I figured she'd just jump in and jump right back out again."

Thunder rumbles in the distance, and more stray raindrops graze my face.

"When did you realize she was in trouble?" I ask, my heart rate quickening as I contemplate that she was just a few yards, maybe even just *feet*, from where I'm sitting now. How could Blake not have noticed things were going wrong? How could he not have gotten to her quickly? Yes, it was dark and the surf was rough, but sitting here now, my vantage point seems so different than the vague images conjured up by the *story* of a drowning. The impact hits me with a thud: This was no story. This was a girl's *life*.

And death.

"I never saw her go under," Blake says quietly. "Like I said, I thought she was basically going to jump in the water then jump out again, so I wasn't thinking, 'I can't let her out of my sight for a second.' It wasn't like that. It's like if somebody goes to refill a drink at a burger joint, you're not going to sit there and watch her the whole time."

Right … except that it was dark and the surf was rough …

"So, you know, she wades into the water, turns around a couple of times and waves at me … "

Blake's voice breaks and he drops his head, emitting a choked sob. I press my palm against his thigh.

"We don't have to talk about this," I tell him in a whisper.

But he holds his head back up, his eyes moist but resolute. "While I was waiting for her, I texted my mom … *Hey, Mom, love you* … then she called me. Does it sound crazy to talk to your mom on a date? I dunno … it's just the kind of relationship we have. Mom called and we talked for a couple of minutes—five tops. I told her we were having a good time, that I'd be home soon, that I'd get up early the next morning to take her to church … "

The waves are crashing closer now, the larger waves spraying us with fine mists of seawater as the tide closes in.

"And when Mom and I finished talking," Blake says, his muscles tensing, "I looked back out into the ocean … and she was gone."

He pauses and looks deeply into my eyes. "Just like that. She was there ... then she was gone."

Tears spring to my eyes. "That's ... that's awful."

He nods and swallows hard. "I stood around for a couple of minutes waiting for her head to pop up out of the water, and when it didn't happen ... "

"You went to get Jamie?" I prod tentatively.

Deep breath. "Yeah."

"And you were still holding Cara's clothes?" I ask.

Blake's jaw drops. *"Jesus,* Anne!"

I sputter, trying to form a response, but nothing really comes out.

"You just don't get it," he says, a touch of contempt in his voice. "I was worried about a girl's *life* and you're wondering if I remember holding on to her clothes or dropping them on the beach?"

"I ... I didn't mean ... "

"Jesus, even the *cops* didn't get that specific," he snaps, and I fleetingly wonder why not. Because Blake's so wholesome? So believable? *Almost too smooth ...*

I meet his eyes for the first time since his story began, suddenly feeling the slightest bit indignant myself. My composure seems to deflate his haughtiness. He stares at the sand and continues his story in an almost whiny voice.

"So I ran to get Jamie," he says.

"Jamie was still with the rest of the group?" I clarify.

Blake nods. "Yeah. He was still at the bonfire, a half a mile or so that way." He points in the direction we walked from.

"So you went and told everybody she was missing?" I

ask, my muscles tensing as I contemplate whether I'm consciously trying to catch him in a lie.

"Yeah," he says. "Then Jamie and I hopped on the jet ski to look for her."

I bite my lip. "And I guess everyone else was looking for her too? Running up and down the beach? Jumping in the water?"

He studies my eyes, then looks out at the sea again.

"No, just Jamie and I went looking. There was no point in a lot of chaos or having other people risk their lives by jumping into the ocean."

But hadn't he just said … ?

I sit up a little straighter. "So … you *didn't* tell everybody right away?"

He shrugs. "I guess not. I guess I just pulled Jamie aside at first and told him."

"But … but if you'd told *everybody*, at least they could have followed you to where she was swimming and stood on the shore helping you and Jamie look for—"

"No, Anne, that's not how it happened." Irritation flashes in his eyes.

Pause. "Okay."

He wipes a raindrop from his brow. "Like I said, I didn't want a lot of chaos, and, you know, for all I knew, maybe Cara had gotten out of the water while I was on the phone with my mom and I just hadn't noticed. I really expected to pass her on the beach when Jamie and I went looking for her, heading back to the bonfire and wondering why in the world I was worried."

His face crinkles like a leaf and his head drops into his hands. He sniffles loudly, then looks up again.

"So, no," he continues, his voice still shaky, "it wasn't like I was screaming and waving my arms like a maniac, shouting for the entire group to start a search party." He shakes his head ruefully, then adds, "Christ, when I say it out loud, I'm like, 'Idiot, why *didn't* you do that?'"

"I get it," I say unconvincingly, not sure if I'm consoling or humoring him, not sure how I feel about *anything* at this point. "It can be hard to know how to interpret a situation," I continue, "and until you're clear on what's going on, you don't want to overreact…"

"Exactly," he says with conviction, the thunder getting closer. *"Exactly.* I didn't want to overreact."

He clamps his lips together to steady his trembling chin. "And you wonder why I feel so guilty."

The seagull swoops onto the water's surface again, then soars into the air.

I'm tempted to stop asking questions now. Just when I start distrusting Blake, he sucks me back into his sympathies; his grief seems so raw, so genuine. But I've come too far to let this story fizzle to a halt. This story's not over yet.

I clear my throat and say, "So you and Jamie looked for Cara on the jet ski?"

He glances at me and looks a bit disoriented, as if his self-flagellation has predictably been the point in the past when people stopped asking him any more questions. *Why are you still yammering?* his expression seems to say. *Don't you know this is where you're supposed to show some respect and shut the hell up?*

Still, he manages to collect himself and answer me.

"Right," he says in a tight voice. "We tore through those waves looking for her. The rip currents were bad that night, but we were flying through the water. My adrenaline was totally pumping by that point. Once it was clear she hadn't gotten back out of the water, man, *that's* when I panicked. I kept screaming at Jamie, 'Hurry, hurry! She's drowning!'"

"But... no signs of her?"

He drops his head. "It felt like we stayed on that jet ski forever. Neither of us wanted to give up. If we went just a little farther, a little deeper, maybe we'd see her bobbing around, thrashing in the water..."

I shiver.

"But... nothing," Blake says, then mindlessly grabs a small shell and flicks it into the ocean. "That's when we ran back to the rest of the group. '*Call 911*,' we yelled. Then the police came, and pretty soon they had the Coast Guard out here, and..."

His face crinkles again and he squeezes tears from his eyes. "That's what happened," he says, his voice breaking.

We sit there for a long time, more ocean spittle peppering our faces, more stray raindrops skittering against our bare arms, more thunder churning ever closer.

So there it is: he's told the whole story now, from start to finish. He said I could ask him anything, and his churlishness at certain points notwithstanding, he's answered my questions. Yes, some details seem odd, but overall, the story hangs together. I mean, people *do* drown, right? Some even in broad daylight with dozens of people around. Cara's circumstances were the worst possible: swimming on a dark, isolated stretch of beach in a rip current. And the police certainly believed Blake. The news clippings made it clear no one ever considered Cara's death suspicious or criminal. Her parents wanted Blake to speak at the memorial service, for crying out loud. Occam's razor: the simplest explanation is usually the right one.

I sit quietly for a few moments trying to collect my thoughts. It's wrenching, torturous, draining to hear a story like this, particularly sitting at the very spot where it happened. I wonder whether a single monster wave swamped Cara that night, or if the rip current pulled her deeper out to sea than she realized, or if she knew exactly what was going on and swam like mad against a too-strong current, flailed for her life, uttered desperate screams that no one could hear amid the crashes of the waves. I shudder.

Of course, Blake can't answer those questions. But there *are* a couple more that maybe he can …

He picks up another small shell and fingers it idly.

"I heard something crazy today," I say quietly.

"What?" Blake asks.

"Just … speculation, stupid gossip … "

"I've heard it all," Blake says, a trace of bitterness in his voice. "You can tell me. What did you hear?"

I squeeze my arms together. "That maybe Cara *wanted* to disappear. I mean … not that she wanted to die, but that she wanted to … disappear."

Blake huffs dismissively. "Sounds like a real genius was floating *that* idea. God, I hope her poor parents haven't heard that one—that's all they need. Why don't people realize when they're running their mouths that actual people with actual feelings are involved?"

"Right, it was stupid."

"So did this rocket scientist toss out a theory about why Cara would want to disappear?" Blake says, his voice dripping with disdain.

A gust of wind suddenly buffets my hair. "Again, it was just stupid speculation ... you know, the typical reason teenage girls disappear. That maybe she was ... pregnant."

I jump as Blake snaps the shell in his fingers in half.

NINETEEN

Crash!

Just as Blake breaks the seashell in half, a jagged, blindingly bright bolt of lightning flashes in the sky, followed by a crack of thunder so loud it makes me tremble.

Then the storm unleashes. Cold, fat raindrops pelt our heads, rain so heavy and torrential that it's hard to see Blake just a few inches away. Within seconds, I'm as soaked as if I've just jumped into the ocean.

Blake grabs my hand. "Let's go!"

We start running down the beach, back toward the car. The boggy sand slows our stride, but Blake keeps pulling me along, tugging roughly at my arm, so roughly that I wonder a couple of times if he's pulled it out of the socket. I'm breathless by the time we reach the car. Blake opens the passenger door for me, then runs around and gets behind the wheel, pulling a hoodie from the back seat and throwing it to me. I dab my face and hair with it, shivering as Blake starts the engine, his windshield wipers flapping furiously. He runs his fingers through his sopping-wet hair.

"Want the hoodie?" I say, rubbing my sore arm.

He grunts in response, his expression dark.

"What's wrong?" I ask as he pulls out of the parking lot.

Silence.

"Blake ... ?"

He drives in silence for a moment, then glares at me from the corner of his eye. "What's *wrong*?" he repeats sarcastically. "Other than feeling like a drowning cat?"

More silence.

"Didn't mean to snap," he finally says.

I study his face, hugging my arms together, as Blake's eyes peer out the windshield. "Why did you freak out when I mentioned that rumor about Cara being pregnant?"

"Because it's bullshit!" he says, making me jump as he pounds his fist on the steering wheel. "You think her mother would get a charge out of hearing that one? As if she hasn't been through enough?"

The mother you supposedly bring flowers to every Sunday?

I set my jaw. "I wasn't talking to Cara's mother; I was talking to *you*. I told you I had some questions, and you told me I could ask you anything."

"Not bullshit! I didn't tell you to ask me bullshit!"

My mouth drops. "How am I supposed to know what's bullshit and what isn't?" I sputter. "I don't know anything about *any* of this! All I know is that I somehow keep getting pulled into other people's drama."

"Yeah, Anne. Keep blaming me for all your issues."

My *issues*?

"You're getting really good at that," he says, snarling. He glares straight ahead, squeezing the steering wheel so hard that his knuckles are white.

"You're driving too fast," I say, but he ignores me.

I shiver again. Who *is* this person? Why do I feel so good about him one minute, so confused the next?

Dr. Sennett's words echo in my head: *Wanting it to be right doesn't make it right.*

I squeeze my eyes shut. Maybe I'm not overthinking anything; maybe I'm *under*thinking. Maybe I'm giving him too many passes.

"You're being rude to me," I say in a brittle voice.

Blake ignores me.

I take a deep breath, then forge on: "I have a question."

More silence—he's still glowering as he speeds toward my house in the pounding rain—but now, his petulance is just emboldening me.

"Does your brother not want you to be alone with me?"

Blake's eyes dart in my direction. What do I see in those eyes? Indignation? Fear? Rage? I don't know, I don't know...

"What are you *talking* about?" he asks as if truly stymied, totally floored by the question. I'm impressed by how quickly he's composed himself. I feel like I'm observing a master class in lying. I've clearly rattled him—his expression a moment ago sure didn't lie—but he recovered in a nanosecond, shifting the focus onto me by trying to make me look ridiculous. Maybe I'm finally figuring out just who Blake is. Maybe I'm understanding him better by the minute.

"When I walked in on you guys the other day at your house—right before you drove me home," I say, my voice surprisingly steady, "he was saying he didn't want you to be alone with . . . with something, with somebody. Was he talking about me?"

Blake tosses his head back and chortles. "Yeah. My little brother doesn't allow me to be alone with my girlfriend."

The word "girlfriend" makes me shudder. The longer I'm with Blake, the clearer I am that I don't want to be his girlfriend.

"Then why did you lie to him?" I persist.

Blake rolls his eyes. "Okay, I'll bite. Lie to him about what?"

"About what you were doing today after school? You told him you had a yearbook meeting."

Blake waves a hand dismissively through the air. He's still acting haughty, but the good news is that he's so busy trying to think on his feet that he's driving slower, no longer whizzing maniacally through the rain-slicked streets.

"*Busted*," he tells me with a sneer. "You caught me lying to my brother. Will you alert the media, or shall I?"

"Why wouldn't he want you to be alone with me?" I say, my voice eerily calm. "And why would you agree to that?"

"Oh, good *god*!" Blake says. "This is the most asinine conversation I've ever had!"

"Left. Turn left!"

"*What?*"

"Left! My street is this left."

Blake's already overshot it, but he turns sharply, making the tires screech in the rain. I hold my breath, wondering if we'll hydroplane or spin out.

Somehow, the car steadies itself, and I exhale slowly through puffed-out cheeks.

"I know where your house is," Blake mutters, and as scary as the turn was, I'm incredibly relieved he's taking me home. I don't know where else I think he might have considered taking me; I'm just so desperate to get home.

Home. I wish I were going to my *real* home. I wish my mom and dad would be there waiting for me. Tears spring to my eyes.

Blake glances at me from the corner of his eye and abruptly pulls alongside the curb, just a couple of houses up from mine.

"*Baby,*" he says.

Damn. He noticed my tears. My heart sinks. Clearly, it's time for Dr. Jekyll to reappear on the scene, full of a fresh set of excuses on behalf of that pesky Mr. Hyde. I don't want to hear his excuses. I don't want to deal with his faux-guilt, or his boyish charm, or his smooth explanations, or whatever tricks he pulls out of his bag to get his way and wriggle his way back into people's good graces. I just want to be somewhere that I can breathe.

Blake touches my hair and I recoil.

He drops his head. "I've been such a jerk."

I swallow hard, shivering in my wet clothes as the rain thrums against the windshield. "Please just take me home."

"This is *not* how I intended this to go, baby..."

And please stop calling me baby.

"Man," Blake says under his breath. "I guess I didn't realize how it would affect me to go back there."

Ah. Time to shift the attention yet again and pull out the trusty ol' sympathy card. What a nice pithy package of several of his manipulative techniques rolled into one.

"Blake, please take me home."

"Baby, I just need you to..."

I suddenly fling my door open, jump out of the car, and start running toward my house. I'm not afraid; I'm just done. I hear him calling after me, but I keep running, rain pelting my face as I pump my arms and pound my soggy shoes into the asphalt.

His shouts are piercing the air—"*Baby! Baby!*"—so I put my hands over my ears as I run through two neighbors' yards to shorten my distance.

Slosh, slosh, slosh go my footsteps through their lime-green lawns.

Home.

I'm almost home...

TWENTY

"What in the world ... "

Aunt Meg, rifling through mail in the kitchen, stares at me wide-eyed as I fling the door open and run inside, dripping on the linoleum and doubling over to catch my breath.

She rushes to my side. "Anne, are you okay?"

I manage to nod, but I'm still too winded to speak.

"Oh my gosh ... let me get you a towel ... "

She runs out of the room, then reappears a minute later with a bath towel and a plush terrycloth robe.

"You've got to get out of those wet clothes," she says, draping the towel around me and peering out the window into our driveway.

"Don't let him inside," I say through heaving breaths.

"Who?" she asks. "I don't see anybody. Who's out there, Anne?"

I press the towel tighter around my shoulders, pull a chair from the kitchen table and collapse into it.

"Who is out there, Anne?" Aunt Meg repeats, her voice verging on full panic mode now.

I press the towel against my shivering arms. "Blake," I say.

She pulls a chair in front of mine, her eyes frantic. "Why are you running from him? What's wrong?"

My cell phone, still on the kitchen table where I left it this morning before heading to school, is blowing up with text messages. I glance at it irritably, then reach over and turn it off.

"Did he hurt you?" Aunt Meg asks, pitching her weight toward me.

"No, no," I say. "I'm sorry I freaked you out, Aunt Meg. I'm fine. Really."

"Then why are you soaking wet? Where have you been?"

I feel a stab of guilt for not telling her where I was going after school. I figured she'd still be at work when I got home, plus it feels so silly to check in with someone at my age, but seeing the worry etched in her face makes my heart sink.

"Were you with Blake?" she asks me.

When I nod, she says in a shrill voice, "I have some serious concerns about him, Anne."

I laugh ruefully. "Problem solved."

"What do you mean?"

I set my jaw defiantly. "I mean I'm done with him."

Aunt Meg's eyes search mine. "Tell me what's happening."

Go ahead. Tell her.

It's the damndest thing... that was my mom's voice in

my head. Crazy, right? Yet I know with every fiber of my being that it's true. So I do what my mother tells me to do. I tell Aunt Meg what's going on.

As we huddle at the kitchen table together, me still shivering in wet clothes with the towel draped over my shoulders, my hair lank with rainwater, I start talking. I tell Aunt Meg that I'd truly started falling for Blake, that he was the only guy I'd ever felt that way about. I tell her that his grief resonated with me, that I felt drawn to his sadness ... but that the more time I spent with him, the more red flags I noticed ... flashes of temper, confusing inconsistencies, smooth manipulations ...

I tell her about the weird vibe between Blake and Jamie, about the notes, about Natalie's strangely convincing denial, about the snippets of conversations I've overheard between Blake and Garrett, about the rumors swirling around about Cara's death ...

Aunt Meg listens intently, leaning closer a couple of times to smooth my wet hair with the palm of her hand.

"So today he took me to the spot on the beach where she drowned," I continue, my tone strangely flat. "He told me I could ask him anything. Well, that's what he said, but there were clearly questions he didn't want to hear. It's crazy how fast he can blow his top."

Aunt Meg's eyebrows knit together. "What do you mean, honey? He didn't get violent in any way, did he?"

I involuntarily shudder. "No," I say softly. "Not really. But he got ... mean. He can be really mean."

"So, did he answer your questions, even the ones he didn't want to hear?"

I hesitate, then nod ambivalently. "Yeah...I guess. Some things are weird...he doesn't seem to remember what he did with Cara's clothes, for instance, and he didn't let the whole group know right away that she was in trouble...A few details seem...sketchy. But he had an answer for everything. Tragedies happen, right? And people don't always react in the heat of the moment in ways that make perfect sense in retrospect. I'm starting to get that he's a jerk, but the story...it makes sense, I guess." I study Aunt Meg's eyes warily. "Cara's aunt, the one you work with...has she ever expressed any...*suspicions* about Blake?"

Aunt Meg shakes her head. "No. All I ever heard was just an acknowledgment of what a terrible tragedy it was. I think her family liked Blake, trusted him...The story seemed perfectly plausible. No one ever questioned it, not that I know of."

"I guess there's no reason anyone would. It sure makes more sense than any other theory out there, like Cara disappearing on purpose. Talk about a long shot. So, yeah...I think I probably believe Blake. I just don't *like* him anymore."

Aunt Meg nods and squeezes my arm gently.

I bite my bottom lip. "Dr. Sennett thinks I'm scared of my future," I say, staring at my hands.

"Your future?" Aunt Meg asks. "What do you mean?"

"She asked about my future, and I told her I couldn't really envision what was *in* it...only what wasn't: Mom and Dad. So maybe I fell for Blake as a way of postponing my future ... that I'm clinging to whatever will keep me from moving forward."

"Wow," Aunt Meg says in a whisper. "Deep."

I wave a hand through the air. "But then I thought, 'That's so silly, so over-dramatic.' Talk about psycho-babble, right? I figured I was just freaked out by the thought of falling for a guy; I mean, I feel ridiculous now, but I've never fallen so hard, so fast, before. I assumed I was overthinking every little thing, kinda subconsciously looking for an escape hatch, because maybe I still wasn't quite ready for a relationship ... "

Aunt Meg's eyes prod me to continue.

"But, of course, the flowers," I say. "Blake telling me he brings Cara's mother flowers every Sunday ... telling *all* of us that." I narrow my eyes. "What a creepy thing to say if it's not true."

"*Hmmmmmm*," Aunt Meg says.

"He also told me he volunteers at the children's hospital. One of our classmates overheard him talking about it, and he said Blake is full of crap."

Aunt Meg and I sit there for a long moment contemplating what it all means.

"Smooth," I finally say. "*Too* smooth."

"So have you talked to him?"

I run a brush through my freshly shampooed hair and sit on the foot of my bed. "Nope," I tell Sawbones, a steady rain still pelting the roof. "He's texted me, like, a zillion times and left some messages. I haven't responded to anything. I guess I'll tell him tomorrow that we need to cool it."

"Do it in public, do it in school," Sawbones says, an alarming hint of urgency in his voice. "I don't want you alone with him."

I scoff lightly. "I'm not afraid of him."

"Are you sure? Sounds like you *have* been afraid a few times."

I finger my parents' rings under my robe. "Not really *afraid*. I mean, I don't think he'd *hurt* me or anything…"

"You know there's more to the drowning story than he's telling you," Sawbones says matter-of-factly.

"I *don't* know that," I say. "A girl jumps in the ocean for a quick swim one night, gets caught in a rip current, tragically drowns. It happens. Her own family—and the *police*, for crying out loud—they all accept that what happened is what Blake said happened. Yes, it was creepy being out there on the beach with him today at the exact spot where it happened, but all the crazy rumors? Cara wanting to disappear? I don't buy any of that. Of course, the bottom line is that I really don't know. But I know one thing: I'm done with Blake."

I take a deep breath, relishing the thought—the exhilarating, liberating notion that's occurring to me just now, this very second—that being done with Blake renders all the other stuff moot. Being done with Blake means being done with Cara, and as crass as that sounds, the very thought makes my muscles relax, makes my stomach unclench, for the first time in weeks.

Being done with Blake means no longer having to deal with his crazy mood swings. Being done with Blake means being totally uninvolved with mysterious notes. Being done with Blake means having no reason to worry about creepy vibes between him and his best friend. Being done with Blake means . . .

Bang! Bang! Bang!

TWENTY-ONE

"Sawyer, I gotta go. Someone's banging on the door."

I don't even wait for him to say goodbye before I end the call and rush out of my room, down the hall toward the front door. Aunt Meg and Uncle Mark are headed there too, both of them speed-walking from the den. We exchange startled glances—whoever is on our porch is practically banging the door down—but none of us slow our stride.

I'm the first one to make it to the front door, but just as I reach for the knob, I feel Uncle Mark firmly take my forearm and pull me back. He peers into the peephole as the banging continues.

"Is it Blake?" Aunt Meg whispers.

Uncle Mark shakes his head.

"Let me look," I say, then nudge him out of the way and peek outside.

"It's Garrett," I tell them. "Blake's brother."

Uncle Mark pulls me back once again and opens the door. Garrett's fist is primed for another whack as the door swings open. He gapes at our faces.

"Garrett?" I say.

He blushes, tossing rain-soaked hair from his face. "Uh … yeah. Hi, Anne. Look, I'm so sorry to bother you folks … "

"Is something wrong?" Uncle Mark asks him.

He rubs the back of his neck. "Uh … no, no … just … dropping by."

"It sure *sounded* like something was wrong," Uncle Mark says, narrowing his eyes. "Why were you banging on the door?"

Garrett blinks several times in quick succession. "Banging? Oh, geez, I'm so sorry, was I banging? How rude. So sorry about—"

"Garrett, do you need to see me?"

All eyes fall on me.

"Uh … if you have a minute, yeah, that would be great," he tells me, his cheeks still bright scarlet.

"We're all right here," Aunt Meg says stiffly. Wow. I've never heard her sound unperky to a guest before.

"It's okay, Aunt Meg," I tell her, working my way out the door. "I'll just talk to him on the porch … "

"It's pouring rain and you're in your robe," she says, pulling me gently back into the foyer. "Inside, please."

"I'm so sorry to disturb you like this," Garrett murmurs. "And again, I feel terrible about the banging. I guess

I thought you might not be able to hear me over the rain. Boy, it's really coming down, huh ... "

"Do you want a towel?" Aunt Meg asks him, surveying his wet clothes and finally stepping back enough to let him inch his way into the foyer.

"A towel? No, no ... But don't worry, I won't sit on your furniture or anything. I'll just stand right here. I have a quick question for Anne about ... school."

Aunt Meg and Uncle Mark exchange wary glances.

"It's fine," I tell them. "We'll just be a minute."

Aunt Meg surveys us both, then says coolly, "Stay in the house please, Anne."

I nod.

"Your uncle and I will be in the kitchen. Right there in the kitchen." She points to the adjoining room with a raised eyebrow, staring at Garrett.

He gulps and nods. "Yes, ma'am."

I've got to admit, I'm embarrassed yet touched at the same time. Who knew Aunt Meg could transform into a mother bear?

She and Uncle Mark hover significantly for a long moment, then walk reluctantly into the kitchen, glancing backwards at us several times en route.

I wave an arm toward the living room couch. "Sure you don't wanna sit?" I ask Garrett.

"No, no," he says, motioning apologetically at his rain-soaked clothes.

The drops are still pounding on the roof.

"What's going on?" I ask him.

After seemingly tossing words around in his head, he finally responds. "I just … I wanted to make sure you were okay."

I study his face. "Why wouldn't I be?"

He twists his fingers into pretzels. "I heard Blake leaving messages on your cell phone. He sounded kind of … frantic."

"I haven't listened to any of his messages," I say.

"Yeah … I guess that's why he kept leaving more. I wasn't eavesdropping, really I wasn't, but he sounded pretty agitated, and I couldn't help but overhear … "

"Garrett, why don't you want me alone with him?"

My question sucks the oxygen from the air. I'm just as surprised as Garrett; I don't even remember forming the words in my head.

"Alone … ?" he asks, shifting his weight nervously.

I stand straighter and cross my arms. "I overheard you. On Sunday, when I was over for dinner. I heard you telling Blake you didn't want him alone with … somebody. You were talking about me, weren't you." It's a statement, not a question.

He squeezes his eyes shut, shifts his weight again, then looks at me again. "Anne, I love my brother. I really do. I just don't always … trust him."

I consider his words, then say, "Because?"

He grips his hands together. "Blake is used to things going his way. I know that sounds crazy after everything he's been through, but it's true. His ego has always gotten a lot of stroking. He … I dunno, there's, like, this air of entitlement. I just like to … keep an eye on him."

I stand there quietly, waiting for him to continue.

"He's always been the golden boy," Garrett says. "Then, when he got cancer, it's like his popularity went into overdrive. He became the town celebrity or something. And my mom ... I mean, he'd always been spoiled, but when he got sick, he ... he could do no wrong, you know what I mean?"

I nod. Yes. Spoiled. Entitled. I've finally started seeing that clearly. How could I have been such an awful judge of character? Was I really that desperate to postpone my future, or maybe to jump-start a new post-parent life? I feel like such an idiot.

"Garrett," I ask him softly, "does Blake volunteer for the children's hospital?"

Garrett's eyes crinkle. "The children's hospital? I mean, he was treated there when he had cancer. Is that what you mean?"

No. It isn't what I mean. I sigh defeatedly.

"Anne, I don't think you should date Blake."

Garrett says these words so fast that it takes me a moment to process them.

"Why is there such a weird vibe between Blake and Jamie?" I ask him.

He averts his eyes and mumbles something I can't understand.

"Why did you rush over here in such a panic?" I continue, then slowly step closer to him. "What did you think had happened with Blake and me?"

"Nothing, nothing," he murmurs. "I didn't know ... "

"Did you think I was ... in danger?"

He doesn't answer, so I answer for him.

"You sure as hell did. You flew over here in a pouring rainstorm like some kind of maniac. You thought something had happened to me. Like . . . like something happened to *Cara* . . . "

He looks at me intently for a moment, then shakes his head roughly. "I don't know what I thought. I didn't know what was going on. I just overheard my brother leaving you some voicemails and sounding upset. I just thought—"

"You're afraid of your brother. You were afraid for *me*."

Garrett's face darkens. "Dammit, Anne, quit putting words in my mouth! I just dropped by to check on you! Stupid, right? I mean, you're a big girl. I don't know what I was thinking. Now your whole family thinks I'm a maniac. Classic. Great. Whatever. It won't happen again. Just . . . just stay away from Blake. Okay?"

But before I can answer, Garrett has opened the front door and dashed back out into the storm, the raindrops pounding his bare head as he runs to his car.

I squint, watching him as he pulls out of our driveway and tears away.

But through the blinding rain, all I can see is a blur.

TWENTY-TWO

I'm in the back seat of our minivan as Dad drives Mom and me to the beach. We've headed out for our annual summer vacation, and I roll down my window to enjoy the breeze. My hair's still long; I haven't cut it yet. I flick it out the window and let it fly through the air. Mom and Dad are murmuring something in the front seat. I can't understand what they're saying, but they're clearly content, smiling and lightly clasping each other's hand. Dad's listening to a Braves game on the radio, and Mom holds a crossword puzzle in her lap, filling out the answers in ink.

I hear a plane overhead and wave at the pilot, whose face I can somehow see clearly. He waves back, a Snoopy-type scarf wrapped jauntily around his neck.

I hum a tune, my hair still blowing in the breeze, then lean up and say, "Hey, it just occurred to me that you guys are here with me."

Dad says, "Of course we are, sweetheart. We're always here."

"Well, this is great!" I say, the full implication finally dawning on me. My parents are here! With me! We're all together! Yes, I know they're dead, but we're together right now, and although I realize I'm dreaming, it's okay, because, oh my god, we're together!

I finger a strand of my hair, then tug on the full length of it. But it isn't long anymore. Now it's short.

Dad pulls into Uncle Mark and Aunt Meg's driveway. He and Mom are still smiling, still relaxed, but I'm getting nervous. Why isn't Dad turning off the engine? Why aren't they getting out of the car?

"Why are you dropping me off? Why can't we all stay here together?" I ask.

"Can't, honey," Dad says. "Sorry."

I'm stammering around trying to object, but Mom is already ushering me out of the car, putting my hand in Aunt Meg's.

"Can I at least hug you before you leave?" I ask her, and her face beams.

"Oh, sweetie, of course you can!"

I hug her tightly, savoring every second. I know it won't last—it can't last, as much as we all want it to—but this moment is sheer perfection.

For one golden moment, I'm in my mother's arms again.

"Morning."

Uncle Mark lifts his cup of coffee as a greeting.

I join him at the kitchen table. "You're usually long gone by the time I get up," I say in my scratchy morning voice, flicking my bedhead bangs off my forehead.

"And look what I've been missing," he teases, sweeping his arm toward my shlumpy flannel pajama pants and wrinkled T-shirt.

"Hi, honey," Aunt Meg says, walking from the stove to present a stack of pancakes. "I cooked this morning."

"Gee..."

As she puts three of the pancakes on my plate, I observe her and Uncle Mark warily. "Is this some sort of intervention?"

I expect a chuckle, but instead, Aunt Meg pulls up a chair by mine and leans into her elbows. "I told Mark you were breaking up with Blake today."

"O-*kay*..." I say. "So he's gonna come to school with me and, like, be my bodyguard?"

Again, nobody laughs. "If need be," Aunt Meg says gravely.

I laugh lightly at their earnestness. "I'll be *fine*," I say. "God, it sounds so stupid to even talk about 'breaking up' with him. How long have I known him? Two weeks?"

"I overheard you talking to his brother last night," Aunt Meg says, then adds breathlessly, "Anne, we're worried about you."

Hmmmmm. It takes me a moment to process being eavesdropped on.

"If you were so worried, why didn't you talk to me as soon as Garrett left?" I ask.

She chews a nail. "I don't know...we weren't sure what to do. We don't want to intrude, or push you away, or—"

"We just want you to know we're here for you," Uncle Mark says quietly. "If you need reinforcements, you know ... we're your guys."

I study Uncle Mark—so steady, so caring, so much like my dad—then smile wanly at him.

"Anne," Aunt Meg says, inching her chair closer, "I had a boyfriend in college. He seemed like a really nice guy at first, but he was actually very controlling and manipulative. It didn't go well when I broke it off; it was a blow to his ego, and he couldn't stand that. So he started stalking me, calling me in the middle of the night commenting on what I'd worn that day, even though I hadn't known he was anywhere around ... things like that."

"And then you married him?" I ask, gesturing toward Uncle Mark, desperate to lighten the mood.

Uncle Mark chuckles gamely, but Aunt Meg stretches her lips into a grim straight line.

"This is no laughing matter," she tells me. "I ended up having to get a restraining order. Honey, Blake ... he reminds me of that guy."

I sigh heavily. "I'm sorry I've got you guys so worried."

"No, no," Aunt Meg insists.

I tap my fingers idly on the tabletop. "I feel like such an idiot. What did I see in him in the first place? Garrett called him spoiled and entitled last night—not that I have to tell *you* that, I guess—but I just thought, you know, 'Duh. Of course. Why didn't I see that right away?' I thought I was a better judge of character."

"Honey, you've been through *so much* lately," Aunt Meg coos, but I shake my head.

"Having your parents die doesn't give you a pass to be stupid. I was such an idiot. And now I'm wrapped up in a bunch of ridiculous gossip and rumors. This is *so* not me."

Uncle Mark gets out of his chair, walks over, and puts his hand on my back. "Annie, you're spectacular," he says softly, and I feel tears welling in my eyes. "You are amazing. You met a guy who's been through a tough time, and your heart went out to him. That's it. Now you're realizing it's not a good fit and you're moving on. You didn't do anything wrong."

A long moment passes.

"But that won't keep Blake from potentially flipping out," Aunt Meg finally says, putting her hand on my knee. "That's what we're worried about."

I swallow hard.

"How about if I take you to school today and pick you up this afternoon?" Uncle Mark says. "I could step inside and give the principal a heads-up … you know, just ask him to keep an eye on things."

I sit up straighter and look him in the eye. "I'll be okay. I promise. I'm afraid if we all start changing things up, it'll make it seem like a big deal. I don't want this to be a big deal. I just want to *not* be dating some guy I've barely been dating anyway. I want to be done with drama."

Uncle Mark considers my words, then nods. "I get that."

"And I'm really not afraid of him," I say. "I'll just tell him when I see him at my locker today that I think we need to cool it. Seven hundred people will be right there with us. And I'll have my cell phone in my purse, so if I need you ... "

"Call us *any time*," Aunt Meg says.

I nod. "I will. And, guys?"

Their eyes prod me on.

"I really am sorry I worried you. I hate to cause you any more trouble than I already have. You know, the whole dumping-myself-on-your-doorstep deal ... "

"Ah, *that*," Uncle Mark says teasingly. "Yeah, when you put it that way, I see that taking you in kinda filled our quota for good deeds. Shall I start keeping a tab of all the extras we're throwing in?"

I giggle at him, and then Aunt Meg starts giggling too. It feels so good to laugh.

"No tabs," Aunt Meg says, her eyes sparkling. "Families don't keep tabs."

———

I pull into the school parking lot, turn off the engine, glance at myself in the rear-view mirror, and take a deep breath. I glance around anxiously at the other cars. No Blake. Good. I'll see him soon enough at our lockers. I'm ready to get this over with, but I'm grateful for a few more minutes of peace.

I get out and start walking toward the entrance, straightening my shirt, then pressing my parents' rings against my chest. I notice a cardinal flying through the air—Mom's favorite bird—and give it a little wave. I finger my short hair and smooth it into place.

"Anne!"

I jump a little, then turn around toward the sound of Melanie's voice.

"Hi, Mel."

She catches up with me and matches my stride. "Well, today's the big day."

We start walking up the steps leading to the entrance. "The big day?"

Melanie smiles mischievously. "The day Natalie unveils the mystery woman."

I force a smile, but truly, I'm so beyond ready to stop talking about this crap. I briefly consider the implications: Will breaking up with Blake mean breaking up with Melanie? Do I *want* it to mean that? After all, it seems like my social life is one big package deal. What happens now that I loathe the package?

I feel guilty for even thinking it. Melanie's been a good friend these past couple weeks. She accepted me from day one, made room for me at her lunch table, took me into the fold. Lauren, too ... even if grudgingly. And really, *I'm* the one who pulled them into the drama with Blake and Jamie, not the other way around. They'd probably jump at the chance to dump *me*. But who knows—maybe no dumping will be required. Maybe I can just settle back into my old familiar role, the one where I live my life and mind my own business, with everybody around me minding *their* own business. Maybe Lauren and Mel and I can keep eating lunch together, only grousing over English Composition tests from now on instead of pondering the intricacies of mystery notes and moody boyfriends. That sounds like heaven right now.

Lauren trots up and joins us.

"Hi," she says. "Think Natalie will have the nerve to leave a note today?"

"Oh, *she* didn't write the notes," Melanie says sarcastically. "She's just the messenger. Remember? Today's the day for the big reveal. Can't wait to see what random name she comes up with. Oh, assuming she gets the fantasy girl's *permission*, of course."

"Here's hoping she just slithers into oblivion," Lauren says as we walk through the school entrance.

"Anne!"

We glance to our left and see Blake rushing toward us. Oh god.

"Hi," I say tersely, without slowing my stride.

"Anne! I tried calling you all night!"

"Yeah, my phone was charging..."

"Anne! I've got to talk to you, baby."

Please stop calling me baby.

Just as we approach Melanie's locker, we see Jamie walking toward us from the other end of the hall. Melanie smiles coyly at him and reaches out to hold his hand. He reluctantly lets her.

"Well, today's the day Natalie reveals the—"

Melanie stops in mid-sentence as we see Natalie running toward us breathlessly, a panicked look in her eyes.

"Speak of the devil," Melanie murmurs.

"Did you hear?" Natalie tells us, clutching her chest as she pants.

We exchange puzzled glances.

"Hear what?" Lauren asks.

She pauses to catch her breath, then looks frantically from one of us to the next before answering:

"They've found Cara's body."

TWENTY-THREE

"*What?*"

"It's true," Natalie repeats. "They've found Cara's—"

Jamie's face turns ashen. He lurches down the hall toward the restroom.

"Jamie!" Blake calls after him, but Jamie keeps running, pushing past the people in his path.

Melanie's brow furrows as she asks me, "Should I go after him?"

We watch him dash into the men's room, the door swinging closed behind him. "You won't be following him in *there*," I say.

Melanie swings toward Natalie, her face contorted with rage. "Why are you doing this? Why are you messing with us?"

"Because she's insane!" Blake bellows, making me jump. "She's a goddamn loon! A nutcase!"

Natalie's face shrivels. "I just thought you'd want to know."

By now, a crowd has gathered, and the guy from the picnic table steps forward, the one who insinuated Blake was full of crap when he talked about volunteering at the children's hospital. "They've found her body," he clarifies, the statement a challenge.

Natalie shrugs, her chin quivering. "That's what her family says. It happened last night. They haven't released the information yet to the—"

"They found her body *last night*," the guy repeats. "And she drowned, what, almost three months ago? During the heat of summer, no less? What exactly do you think is left of her body at this point?"

Natalie shakes her head pitifully, seeming to shrink before our eyes.

The guy turns to the crowd, now holding court. "The ocean water's around eighty degrees right now; it was even hotter over the summer. You think a body just drifts around pristinely in conditions like that? Even assuming the sharks haven't devoured—"

"Stop it!" I say, clapping my hands over my ears.

Blake charges the guy, butting him with his chest. "You shut the hell up!" he shouts.

The guy backs off and presents his palms as stop signs. "*She's* the one who started this," he says nervously, gesturing toward Natalie. "I'm just pointing out a few scientific—"

"I don't know what exactly they found," Natalie sputters. "Maybe a bone, or her bathing suit, or a piece of jewelry or something...I don't know. I just know from a *very reliable source* that her body—some part of her body, something identifiable—has been recovered." She looks at us pleadingly. "I'm not just making all this up!"

"The hell she's not!" Blake says. "She's always looking for ways to worm her way into my life. God, I couldn't get through a single *day* in the hospital without her bringing me a plate of mushy brownies, or some corny card, or a stupid stuffed bear, or—"

Natalie drops her face in her hands, emits a piteous moan, then runs down the hall.

I stare at Blake evenly. "What a cruel thing to say."

His hands fly in the air. "It's true! And now I'm supposed to sit back while she makes my life hell, peck-peck-pecking at me until she gets some little morsel of attention?"

"Shut up, Blake," I mutter, then run down the hall after Natalie.

I follow her into the women's restroom, reaching her just as she's about to slam shut the door of a stall. I block the door from closing.

"Natalie..."

A couple of girls applying lipstick in front of the restroom mirror glance at us and discreetly slip out.

"Just leave me alone," Natalie wails, trying to force the door closed against my weight. "Please."

"I just want to talk to you a minute," I say, trying to sound soothing. "Please?"

She drops her hands defeatedly to her side and peers at me through tear-stained eyes. "You wanna talk to somebody? Go talk to your *boyfriend*."

I bristle. "He's not my boyfriend. I'm not seeing him anymore. He's a jerk. I hate the way he talks to you."

She laughs ruefully through her tears. "It's true. Everything he said is true." She waves. "'Hi, everybody. I'm the pathetic sap in love with a guy who can't even stand the sight of me.' I'm not crying because of what he said; I'm crying because it's *true*."

I peer into her face. "Except him accusing you of writing those notes and intentionally stirring up things about the drowning. *That's* not true... right?"

She dissolves into a fresh wave of tears and shakes her head vigorously from side to side. "I didn't write the notes. And I wasn't lying this morning. I was just repeating what I was told... from a *very reliable source*."

"*Who,* Natalie?" I press. "What's going on? And why does this person keep singling out Jamie instead of Blake?"

She squeezes in her lips and speaks in a stronger voice than before. "She thinks Jamie's really bad news. She's scared of him."

The words bounce around in my head for a moment. "But *why*? Why Jamie?"

Natalie pulls a lock of hair behind her ear. "She won't tell me. Obviously it has something to do with Cara, but I don't know what..."

"*Why?*" I demand. "Why are you so sure it has something to do with Cara?"

Natalie looks at me steadily. "Because she's Cara's best friend."

I hand Natalie a tissue and she limply accepts it, dabbing at her eyes.

We're sitting on the cold bathroom tile now, our backs pressed against the wall. The first-period bell has rung, but we've ignored it. We have the bathroom to ourselves, and I'm not missing this opportunity to reach out to Natalie— not only because she's finally filling in some missing pieces, but because I'm afraid to leave her alone. She's so fragile, so wounded ... a hollowed-out shell who's decided that Blake—egomaniac *Blake*, of all people—holds the key to her self-worth, to her happiness, to her sense of belonging. I can't help but wonder what would have happened if she'd been alone in the bathroom. Would she have shattered the mirror and slashed a piece of jagged glass against her wrist? Blake was so cruel to her, so gratuitously cruel. How *dare* she give him the power to crush her soul?

"What was her name again?" I ask Natalie now, squeezing my knees against my chest.

"Rebecca," Natalie says. "I've known her since Blake and Cara started dating two years ago. I didn't really know anybody from Cara's school, but I started following a bunch of them on Snapchat and Twitter, figuring out where the parties were or where they might be hanging out."

She glances at me to gauge my reaction. "Do I sound like a stalker?"

"Yeah," I admit, and we laugh lightly.

"I didn't mean to be," Natalie says, peering into space.

"I knew I didn't stand a chance with Blake. I've always been a nobody, and he's always been, like, a *god* almost. It just made me feel good to be *near* him, to be his friend. At least I *thought* I was his friend..."

"Why would you want to be friends with somebody who treats you like crap?"

Natalie shrugs.

"Would you, like, *stop* it?" I say, and she smiles wanly.

Then she looks at me shyly and asks, "Why are you being so nice to me? I was horrible to you that night at the bonfire. I feel really—"

"It's okay," I say. "Who cares. It's over. Tell me more about Rebecca and Cara."

Natalie takes a deep breath and continues:

"So Rebecca and Cara had been best friends since, like, first grade. Rebecca was just crushed when Cara died. It killed her. And she's been weird about Jamie ever since."

"So, like, she thinks Jamie drowned her or something?"

Natalie thrums her fingers on her knee. "She wouldn't say. She said she *couldn't* say. She just seemed to know something that nobody else did. All I know is that while everybody else was whispering rumors about *Blake*, she was focused on Jamie. That suited me fine; I liked that she knew what a good guy Blake is. I knew he could never hurt anybody."

I raise an eyebrow. "He hurts *you* all the time."

She shakes her head. "Just because I'm a pest who won't leave him alone," she says, and my fists clench at her maddening insistence on giving Blake a pass for *everything*, for hating herself rather than him.

"Blake loved Cara, he really did," Natalie continues. "They talked about getting married. He was crazy about her, and everybody knew it. *Rebecca* knew it. I don't think she had anything against Blake at all; she knew he worshiped Cara. It was *Jamie*. She never would tell me why she was so mad at Jamie."

"Was Rebecca at the bonfire the night Cara drowned?" I ask, and Natalie shakes her head quickly.

"She couldn't go. She had something going on with her family. That always killed Rebecca too—I think she felt like Cara would still be here if she'd gone that night."

A bored voice starts droning announcements over the loudspeaker, but Natalie and I ignore the noise.

"Everybody keeps telling me how Jamie has always practically idolized Blake," I say, and Natalie nods in agreement. "But that's not what I see. Jamie acts like he *hates* him. There's all this tension between them, yet they seem like they're joined at the hip."

Natalie *mmmms* her agreement. "Jamie got really hot over the summer. He was kinda scrawny before, kinda wimpy, really shy. Nobody paid much attention to him. He was always in Blake's shadow."

"That's what I've heard," I say. "And that would explain why Blake might suddenly resent Jamie—I'm finally getting that he can't stand sharing the spotlight—but it wouldn't explain why Jamie is so hostile toward *Blake*. And that's what it is: hostility."

"Trust me, I've asked Rebecca a thousand times what's up," Natalie says. "We really got close while Blake and Cara were dating, and we got *extra* close after Cara died. She's cried on my shoulder more times than I can count. But getting any specifics from her—why she hates Jamie—she won't say."

"Jamie was supposed to speak at Cara's memorial service," I say, and Natalie nods.

"I know. That *killed* her. She was so upset, and so relieved when he ended up staying in his seat. She never, you know, accused him of hurting her or anything, but *something* happened before Cara died that turned her against him. Then, when I told Rebecca that Jamie was dating Melanie, she … freaked out. She felt like she had to protect her, even though she doesn't know her. The night after the bonfire, when you guys had gone on another date, I drove her to Melanie's house so she could put a note in her mailbox. She didn't show it to me, and she didn't tell me it was anonymous. You know, I'm not an idiot, and I figured she was trying to let Melanie know that Jamie was bad news, but I didn't know any specifics. Then, when they kept dating, she asked me to put a couple more notes in Melanie's locker."

I narrow my eyes. "You weren't tempted to peek?"

Natalie shrugs. "The envelopes were sealed. Plus, I'm not really that interested in Jamie or Melanie."

I can't help shaking my head ruefully at her guilelessness.

"I didn't know the earth would practically explode when Blake saw me putting one of the notes in Melanie's locker," Natalie says. "I called Rebecca right away and asked if I could tell everybody that she was the one writing them. She said she'd think about it and let me know. Then she called me this morning with the news about Cara's body being found."

"Hmmmmmmm..."

Natalie studies me cryptically. "What are you thinking?"

I clasp my hands together. "Sounds like a good way to deflect your question. To keep from having to answer it."

"No," Natalie insists, "she said she'd just gotten off the phone with Cara's mother..."

"But a body being found after months in the ocean in the height of summer?" I say. "Really? Like I said, it sounds like a good way to get you to change the subject, or..."

Natalie leans closer. "Yes?"

I stare into space. "Or to try to bring things to a head."

TWENTY-FOUR

"Anne!"

I suck in a breath. Blake has jumped out from behind a wall as I'm walking from the restroom to my class.

"Where have you *been*?" he asks, gripping my forearm tightly.

I glance at my arm. "Let go, please."

"What?"

I set my chin. "Please let go of my arm."

He tosses his hands in the air. "Jesus *Christ*! Would you just tell me what the hell is going on?"

I furrow my brow. "Why aren't you in class?"

"Why aren't *you*?"

I cock my head to the side. "Have you been waiting on me?"

He shakes his head slowly, one of his many mannerisms

that, I've come to recognize, signals his incredulity at how stupid the people around him are. "So it's a big shock that I'd be interested in knowing what Nutcase Natalie had to say?"

"If you're interested in knowing what she has to say, you can ask her yourself. You might want to curb the cruelty; now that you need something from her, it would be a good time to trot out the charm."

I resume my walk toward class.

Blake huffs and follows me, his sneakers pounding the tile. "So now *I'm* the bad guy? After the crap she's been pulling? And don't think I believe her for a minute: 'Oooooooohhh, they found the body. Everybody look at me! I know something you don't!'" He's using the same high-pitched, sing-song voice he used when he talked about the things Natalie brought him to the hospital, pouring on generous slatherings of ridicule and contempt. I want to hurl. I keep walking, staring straight ahead.

"Jesus, Anne, do you have any idea how it affects me to hear things like that about Cara?"

I stop and face him. "Enough, Blake. I'm onto your bag of tricks. I know it's time to whip out the poor-pitiful-me card."

His jaw drops. "Like I'm *faking* my feelings about Cara?"

I ponder the question, then say, "Maybe."

I resume walking, and he trots after me, getting a little breathless. "Christ, Anne, talk about cruel! Why are you being so cold? Why won't you answer my calls? Is this the price I pay for getting a little rattled the first time I go back to the scene of my girlfriend's death?"

I keep walking. I'm *so* done.

"Anne!"

Still walking, still ignoring him.

"Don't you get how much I love you?" he asks, his voice suddenly plaintive.

I roll my eyes and keep walking.

"You know what?" Blake says as I near my classroom, his stride still matching mine. "I thought I appreciated Cara, but I didn't even come *close* to understanding what an amazing girl she was until I met *you*. I figured every girl was like her: sweet and caring and loyal. Now I know how hard it is to find someone like—"

I reach my classroom and face him one last time before walking inside. "See ya."

It's only as I'm halfway inside the door that I hear his parting shot:

"*Bitch.*"

I take a deep breath, then walk toward the cafeteria table.

I've been able to avoid discussions all morning, hiding my head in a book between classes to feign studying, but there's no avoiding questions at a lunch table. I considered skipping lunch altogether, but I don't want to fuel the flames by acting sketchy. Still, I don't want to tell Melanie and Lauren about my conversation with Natalie. Yes, I guess both of them—especially Melanie—have as much of a right as I do to know who wrote the notes, and for all I know, Natalie's already told them—but I don't want to get drawn into more gossip. I don't want to talk about Cara. I don't want to talk about Blake. I don't want more drama.

But I take one look at their faces when I reach the lunch table and realize that's not in the cards. Their eyes are wide, their muscles tense.

"Jamie's gone," Melanie informs me gravely before I even sit down.

"What?"

"He's gone! Remember when he went to the bathroom after Natalie told us about Cara's body? He must have left the building from there. Nobody's seen him since. He hasn't been in any of his classes."

"O-*kay*," I say, settling into my seat and placing my tray on the table. "I guess he was sick. He sure *looked* sick."

"He didn't look sick," Melanie says. "He looked terrified." She bites a nail and continues. "I *knew* I should have gone to him when he ran to the bathroom. I *knew* Natalie's message pushed him over the edge."

"What are you saying?" I ask slowly.

"Nobody realizes how sensitive Jamie is," Melanie says, pushing her fingers anxiously through her hair. "He's just now started confiding in me, letting me know how much he cared about Cara and how devastated he was when she died."

"Blake got all the attention, naturally," Lauren says bitterly. "Blake *always* gets all the attention."

"But the drowning really did a number on Jamie too," Melanie continues. "He still hasn't gotten over it. He can't talk about it without crying. He's like a baby in my arms every time I try to get him to open up." Her trembling hand hovers over her mouth. "I *knew* I should have gone to him."

"Call him," Lauren says. "I'll spot you so you won't get caught on your cell phone."

"I've tried," Melanie says, now on the verge of tears. "My calls keep going straight to voicemail."

Her eyes dart from Lauren's face to mine, then back again.

"I'm going to his house," she tells us firmly.

"Now?" Lauren asks, but Melanie has already jumped up from the table, leaving her tray behind, and bolted out the door.

"Call us?" Lauren shouts out to her weakly, but Melanie doesn't respond.

She's long gone.

———————

"So, Natalie's full of shit."

I look at Lauren evenly.

"My brother-in-law works the cop beat for the *Hollis Island Tribune*," she continues. "I texted him after Natalie's bombshell, and he said there's nothing to it. The dead girl's body has not been recovered."

"Mmmmmm."

Lauren stares at me long enough to make me squirm. "But then, you already knew that," she says, drawing out each word.

I feign surprise. "What do you mean?"

"Everybody knows you were holed up with Natalie in the bathroom during first period."

I roll my eyes. "Geez. How about what I had for breakfast? Is that a hot topic of conversation, too? What else does 'everybody' know?"

"That you dumped Blake," Lauren responds coolly.

I drop my head back and groan. "Can I just have an uneventful day of school?"

"Not when you kick it off by dumping the school stud. The first smart thing you've done since you got here, in my humble opinion."

"How would anybody know I dumped him?" I ask, genuinely curious.

"Ah, poor, innocent, naïve Anne. Allow me to introduce you to the ways of the world, wherein juicy school gossip becomes viral at the approximate speed of light."

"Well, the paparazzi can just go on their merry way," I say through gritted teeth, "because from this point onward, I plan to be excruciatingly un-newsworthy."

Lauren motions behind me. *Or not,* she mouths.

I turn around and see Blake walking toward me.

"I need to talk to you," he says as he reaches me.

"Hey Blake, have you heard from Jamie?" Lauren asks him. "The word on the street is he's MIA."

Blake flashes her a look of intense annoyance and Lauren cuts her eyes at him. Blake turns his attention back to me. "Please. Give me five minutes."

"I don't want to talk, Blake," I say.

"Please, Anne…"

"Leave her alone," Lauren snaps at him. "There's nothing

to talk about anyway. Natalie was lying. Cara's body hasn't been—"

"Shut up!"

Blake spits the words at her so venomously that our jaws drop. "You have no right to even utter Cara's name!" he says, a vein in his neck bulging.

Then he looks at me. "You think you can dump *me*? You were never anything but sloppy seconds to begin with! And don't believe what people say about you two looking alike, by the way; she was *so* much hotter than you. Do you honestly think I would've given you a second glance if the love of my life hadn't died? God, to think I took you there yesterday … brought you to the place where she took her last breath. You don't deserve to so much as—"

"Blake."

Garrett has walked up behind his brother, uttering his name with eerie calm as he puts a hand on Blake's shoulder. "Enough, dude. Let's go eat our lunch."

Blake shakes off his brother's hand, his face red and mottled.

"Do you know she has the nerve to think she's somebody special?" Blake tells him, nodding his head at me with a quick jerk. "She thinks she's some kind of goddamn—"

"*Dude.*"

Garrett looks at me apologetically, then pulls his brother away. Blake resists at first but then reluctantly starts following, turning around a couple of times en route to glare at me menacingly.

"Oh my god," Lauren mutters.

My heart is pounding, but I aim for blasé. "I sure know how to pick 'em, huh?"

Lauren leans closer. "Anne, this is no laughing matter. He looked like his head was about to explode."

"Well, that would be *one* way to get rid of him."

"I've never trusted that guy," Lauren continues, her voice low. "He's so damn wholesome, so nauseatingly fake-humble … yet he still somehow manages to hog every crumb of attention within a fifty-mile radius. You know, I couldn't help thinking he was secretly loving the attention after Cara died. It sounded too awful to even say it, but I truly got that vibe … everybody giving him a wide berth like he was some kind of freakin' celebrity, everybody whispering about him and tiptoeing around him, so careful not to shake his little world or upset his delicate sensibilities … He was loving it. He *was*. I could tell. He was eating it up."

Lauren inches her head closer toward my face. "He's a world-class creep," she concludes definitively. "Let me walk you to your car after school."

I feel ridiculously high-maintenance, but my shoulders relax at the suggestion. "You're sure you don't mind?"

She smiles warmly—maybe the first authentic smile she's really given me. "I've got your back," she says.

———

"And I have to study tonight, but I'll call you after I get back from the—"

Lauren's phone interrupts her, ringing as she walks me to

my car after school. She continues walking for the first moment or two, then stops dead in her tracks. I stop, too, and watch her eyes widen. I hear her incredulously blurting, "When?" "How many?" "Where?"

When she ends the call, she stands motionless for a moment, looking frozen in place.

"*What?*" I prod.

She blinks several times and finally meets my gaze.

"It's Jamie," she says.

"What about him?"

She blinks again, stares into space, and says:

"He tried to kill himself."

TWENTY-FIVE

"Oh, god!"

Lauren and I sweep Melanie into an embrace, her body shaking, as we enter the hospital waiting room.

We disentangle and Melanie opens her mouth to speak, but nothing comes out.

"Here," Lauren says, taking her arm and guiding her to a chair. She lowers Melanie into the chair, then Lauren and I sit beside her.

"What happened?" Lauren says, her voice lowered even though no one else is in the room.

Melanie blinks back tears. "I ... I ... "

Lauren grabs a tissue from the end table and hands it to her. Mel clutches it tightly.

"Take your time," Lauren says.

We wait a couple of moments, then Melanie looks at us, one after the other.

"I went to his house during lunch," she says. "His mom answered the door; she said he came home not feeling well and had been asleep ever since. She seemed ... I dunno, a little worried, but not excessively. Still, we talked for a long time. We'd only met a couple of times before, just to say hi, so we must have spent over an hour just getting to know each other. She told me how depressed Jamie had been since Cara died, that they'd gotten really close while she and Blake were dating, and that it destroyed him not to be able to save her."

Melanie dabs her tear-stained cheeks with the tissue.

"So, you know, we talked mostly about him, but his mom asked me a few questions about myself, and we just kind of chit-chatted awhile."

"Yes?" I say.

"Then ... it was weird, because both of us seemed to get a weird feeling at the same time ... we decided his mom should poke her head in his bedroom and check on him ... "

My heart clutches. What the hell are we about to hear?

Melanie starts sobbing. Lauren holds her hand while I offer the tissue box.

"She called me from upstairs," Melanie says, her voice jagged with sobs. "I ran up there, and his mom was trying to shake him awake. She couldn't figure out why it was so hard to wake him up. He's a really light sleeper."

She wrings her hands in her lap.

"I went over and tried to help her. We were both calling his name, louder and louder."

Lauren and I exchange anxious glances.

"Then his mom pulled the sheets off him, and that's when we saw the bottle..."

We lean in closer and narrow our eyes.

"He'd taken a bottle of pills, something his mom had been prescribed after her knee surgery," Melanie says, shaking with more sobs. "She screamed, 'Call 911! Call 911!' So I called, and she just kept shaking him while we waited for the ambulance to get there, but we couldn't wake him up, then they came, and..."

She drops her head and shakes it, still weeping.

"What do the doctors say?" I ask, stroking her hair. "Is he gonna be okay?"

She shrugs. "I don't know anything. His parents are with him. I just keep waiting for somebody to tell me what's going on."

While Lauren continues to console Melanie, I slip to the other side of the room and send Natalie a private Facebook message giving her my phone number and a message:

"I don't have your phone number. Please call me immediately at 555-0127. URGENT."

An hour passes with no more information than we had when Lauren and I first ran to the hospital. But a bigger crowd has gathered in the waiting room, including Aunt Meg and Melanie's parents.

I'm willing myself to sit calmly, trying not to fidget other than pressing my parents' rings against my chest. Natalie called me within ten minutes of getting my message and said I'd hear back from her shortly, but so far, nothing. Oh well. I've begged her to do me a favor, and if she's doing it, it's no doubt taking a while. She told me she wasn't sure she'd be able to come through, but that she'd try. What more can I ask? Nothing to do now but wait.

Aunt Meg wanders over to my chair. "So tell me again how Blake and Jamie are connected ... ?"

"Best friends," I say, then realize how ridiculous that sounds. Jamie isn't Blake's best friend. Jamie hates Blake. But there's no need to delve into all the nuances with Aunt Meg. "Best friend" works for now. Which makes me wonder if Blake should know what's going on ...

Who knows. But he won't hear it from *me*.

I suck in my breath when I see Natalie at the door of the waiting room, nervously peeking inside. She locks eyes with me urgently, and I rush out into the hall.

Once I'm in the hall, I realize she isn't alone. A girl is with her, a pretty girl with light freckles and light brown hair. I breathe a sigh of relief. Natalie came through.

"Hi," the girl says to me.

I don't need an introduction to respond.

"Hi, Rebecca."

"Please tell me what you know."

Rebecca fingers the straw of her drink nervously, then sneaks a glance at me.

"Wow," she tells me. "You really *do* look a lot like Cara."

She and Natalie and I have gone to the hospital cafeteria so we can talk privately. A few other people mill around with trays, but as is always true in hospital cafeterias, everyone is immersed in their own thoughts, their own dramas. Natalie, Rebecca, and I have complete privacy.

"I'm really torn," Rebecca says, still picking at her straw. "I don't want any of this to get back to Cara's parents."

"Rebecca, I don't want you to break any confidences," I say, leaning into my forearms on the table, "and there's certainly no reason for me to go around talking about other people's business. But Jamie just tried to *kill* himself. Whatever's going on is hugely intense. I don't know if I can help, but I've got a strong sense that things will just get worse if we don't get all the cards on the table."

Rebecca takes a deep breath, exhaling through an O in her mouth, and as I sense her wavering, I lean in even closer.

"Jamie's life might depend on what you know," I say gravely.

A look of insouciance flickers across her face. "Maybe he *should* die."

Natalie and I lock eyes, then turn back to Rebecca.

"Why would you say that? Did he have something to do with Cara's death?"

She considers my question, then shrugs. "It's nothing

I can prove. That's why I never said anything. All it would have done is hurt Cara's parents. It would have killed them."

My eyebrows knit together. "So you think he drowned her?" I persist.

She thinks for a second, then nods quickly, as if to commit to it before she changes her mind.

"Wow," Natalie says. "I just thought you considered him a creep. I didn't know you thought he *killed* her."

Rebecca sneaks a cautious glance at us. "Like I said, I couldn't prove anything, particularly since she's never been found. That's why I planted the rumor about the body being recovered. Jamie knew that if they found Cara's body..."

"If they did, then *what*?" I say.

"They'd know he had a motive for killing her."

The cafeteria din sounds like a discordant symphony: trays clanging, silverware clinking, drink machines whirring. But Natalie and I are totally focused on Rebecca. I feel like I haven't taken a breath in five minutes.

"Why? What would they have found?" I ask her slowly.

She chews her bottom lip. "Please don't say anything. Like I said, this would kill her parents."

I nod my compliance.

Rebecca clasps her hands together, then says, "She was pregnant."

Natalie and I draw in quick breaths.

"No wonder Blake freaked out when I told him people were gossiping about that," I say.

"No, no. It was Jamie's baby, not Blake's," Rebecca clarifies. "She told him the night of the bonfire."

I take a moment to absorb the shock. "How do you know she told him?" I ask. "I thought you weren't there."

Rebecca sniffles and blinks back tears. "She'd just found out. She and Jamie had been seeing each other on the down low for a few weeks ... just a few weeks. She felt terrible about cheating on Blake, but I think she was starting to feel a little smothered. It's like Jamie was her escape hatch. So she took the pregnancy test ... "

"How did she know it was Jamie's baby?" I ask. "Why couldn't it have been Blake's?"

Rebecca pauses, glancing anxiously around the room. She says in a lowered voice, "Blake can't have kids. He told Cara the chemotherapy he took when he had cancer left him infertile."

Natalie's eyes widen. "Oh god."

"Plus, she hadn't been with Blake in a while ... not like that," Rebecca says. "She didn't want to hurt Blake, but she was trying to pull back a little, to get a little space. She didn't want to hurt Jamie either. She wasn't using him, she was just ... I dunno, she was just very confused. She was a really sweet girl."

She stresses her last sentence, searching our eyes for validation that we believe her.

"Still," she goes on, "her parents would have been crushed to know she was pregnant. She didn't tell them. She didn't tell anybody but me. She was frantic; she didn't know what to do. But she said she was going to tell Jamie that night at the bonfire."

More clanging, more clinking, more whirring. Everything going on around me is like a blur, a big, noisy blur.

"So you think he killed her?"

Her jaw hardens. "I think he's a horrible, spineless coward. He couldn't face Blake's disapproval, and he couldn't face being a father. He couldn't face any of it."

I shake my head impatiently. "But Blake is the one who was alone with Cara when she went into the water," I insist. "At least that's what he *said*."

Rebecca ponders my words, then says, "I've always wondered if Blake was covering for Jamie. It's hard to believe... he loved Cara so much, and he wouldn't have known about the baby—*Jamie* sure wouldn't have told him—but maybe Jamie killed her, then convinced Blake that Cara had died in some kind of freak accident and begged Blake to keep his secret."

"No. *No*," I say firmly. "I was with Blake at the beach yesterday, right where it happened. He told me everything. Who knows if it's true, but... if he *did* tell me the truth, then he and Cara were alone when she went into the water. Jamie was still at the bonfire with the others."

"And maybe Blake is telling the truth," Rebecca says. "Everybody *else* believed it. I figured people would ask questions, you know, the police or whoever, and I knew I'd tell the truth if anybody asked. But..."

Her eyes fall. "Nobody ever did."

"Everybody believed Blake," I say, more to myself than

anyone else. Uncle Mark's words ring in my head yet again: *almost too smooth.*

"Still," Rebecca adds, "as soon as I heard that Cara died that night, I thought, 'That bastard. She told him and he killed her.' He could have gotten her alone on the beach, you know. I'm sure there was lots of coming and going. Nobody would have noticed if they'd slipped off together; it was just a big crowd of people. Deep down in my heart, that's what I thought when I heard she'd died. I thought, 'Jamie killed her.'"

I shake my head. "I know I've only known Blake a few weeks," I say, "but I've seen lots of different sides of him. He can fly into a rage on a dime. He can be very manipulative. He can be controlling."

"*Controlling,*" Rebecca says, looking intrigued. "That's how Cara started describing Blake toward the end."

"He doesn't like to lose," I say, in such a quiet voice that the other girls lean in.

"What did you say?" Natalie asks.

I pause, then answer:

"Jamie's not the only one who had a motive to kill Cara."

TWENTY-SIX

"They think he's gonna make it."

Rebecca, Natalie, and I glance up, disoriented at the sound of a new voice jumping into our intense conversation.

Melanie is standing at our cafeteria table with Lauren and two adults. "The doctors said they're pretty sure he'll pull through," Melanie says, her face easing into a relieved smile.

"Oh, Mel, that's ... that's wonderful," I say.

"These are Jamie's parents," she tells us, and we all smile and murmur condolences.

"We're headed right back up," his mother says. "He's still sedated, so he won't wake up for a while. We thought we'd take a moment to grab a cup of—"

"Who's with him now?" I ask anxiously, then blush for seeming so presumptuous. "I mean ... "

"Blake's sitting with him now," his mother says. "He got here as soon as he—"

I spring from my chair and run out of the cafeteria.

———————

"*Come on, come on, come on...* "

I stare at the elevator lights, practically willing the doors to open. I considered taking the stairs, but running six flights would probably take longer than waiting on the elevator. Still, the wait is killing me...

Ding!

The light flashes and the doors open. It takes every ounce of self-restraint I have to keep from pushing past the people getting off, but I manage to wait.

Well, almost... When the last two people are about to exit, I squeeze past them into the elevator. One of them gives me a dirty look, but I ignore it. I push six.

"*Come on, come on, come on...* "

I've never noticed before how slowly elevators move, especially when stopping at other floors. I feel like begging the newcomers to hurry up, hurry up, but of course I just stand there fidgeting instead, pressing my parents' rings against my chest.

Finally, finally, the elevator reaches my floor. A couple of other people are getting off here too, but at this point I dispense with all formality and simply run out of the elevator, pushing past them.

And I just keep running.

I run down the hall, past the waiting room I was in just a

few minutes ago. By the time I reach the nurses' station, I'm breathless.

"Jamie Stuart's room, please," I say, panting.

As the nurse presses a few computer keys, I see someone familiar in my peripheral vision. I turn my head for a better look.

"Garrett—"

"Room 626," the nurse tells me.

"Anne. What's going—"

"Let's go!"

I grab his arm and bolt toward Jamie's room, pulling Garrett in my wake.

Once I get to his room, I fling open the door and see Blake.

He's holding a pillow over Jamie's face.

TWENTY-SEVEN

"*No!*"

My scream is guttural, primal, more tortured than any sound I've made since I learned my parents had just been killed.

"*Get away from him!*" I screech at the top of my voice.

Blake looks at Garrett and me, startled for a nanosecond, then indignant.

"For god's sake, I was just adjusting his—"

A couple of nurses run into the room and I point at Blake. "He was trying to kill him," I say breathlessly. "He was holding a pillow over his face."

Blake's jaw drops dramatically. "Are you *crazy?*"

"It's true!" Garrett tells the nurses. "I saw it too. My brother was trying to smother him."

"Call security," one nurse tells the other as she bustles to Jamie's bedside. "I want you all to leave immediately," she tells the rest of us.

Blake sputters, "This is the most insane accusation I've ever—"

"Out!" the nurse barks.

Blake glares at me as we walk out the door, and I glare back.

Once we're back in the hall, he holds his composure for just a second before his eyes start darting around.

"Blake, I know all about—"

But he's not listening.

He starts tearing down the hall, pumping his arms and pounding his feet as if his life depended on it.

———————

"Officers, this is all a big mistake."

Blake is smoothing his hair as the security officers stop him in mid-stride.

One officer radios for backup, and another asks Garrett and me what's going on.

"My brother tried to kill that patient," Garrett says, his forceful voice betrayed by only the slightest tremor. "He killed his girlfriend over the summer, and the patient in that room knows it—it's Jamie Stuart, his best friend, and Jamie helped him cover up the crime. Jamie just tried to commit suicide, and Anne and I walked in on Blake trying to smother him with a pillow."

"That is *ludicrous*!" Blake howls. "This is all a big misunderstanding. A huge, ridiculous—"

Garrett starts sobbing and falls into my arms.

———————

"Drink, drink."

Aunt Meg and I have led Garrett to a chair in the waiting room and are trying to get him to sip some water. He's shaking so hard, he knocks the bottle from Aunt Meg's hand.

"They need to arrest me too," he tells us in a spent voice, his eyes haunted. "I knew. I covered it up for him."

"What are you talking about? You're the one who caught him!" Aunt Meg says. "You *saved* Jamie."

Garrett shakes his head. "I knew about Cara. Not at first ... not until a few weeks ago. Jamie told me. The guilt was eating him alive. Cara told Blake that night at the bonfire that she was pregnant ... pregnant with Jamie's baby. She said she wanted Blake to hear it first, before she told anyone else, even Jamie. I confronted Blake after Jamie told me. At first he denied it, but after a while, he confessed that he'd blown his top that night, and ... " Garrett can't quite spit out the words.

"But he told me it was an accident," he continues. "I wanted to believe that so badly ... "

He drops his head into his hands and sobs.

"How did he kill her?" I ask.

"He slammed a rock over her head. At first, he told me that she'd accidentally fallen against the rock—that he'd shoved her out of anger after he found out about her and Jamie, after he found out she was pregnant—and that she'd stumbled and fallen. But then one night a few days ago—one night that he was furious at me for trying to keep him away from Anne—he spit it out. Actually *bragged* about smashing the rock over her head. He was almost proud, you know? Like she deserved it. Like he had every right to decide whether she lived or died. She'd messed with his ego. He couldn't handle it."

Garrett's teary eyes narrow as he gazes into space.

"He has, like, the world's craziest sense of entitlement. He's always been that way... but once he got cancer, he was the golden boy who could do no wrong. Nobody questioned him anymore. The brakes were off."

I shake my head. "But Jamie wouldn't have just gone along with him... would he?"

Garrett squeezes his hands together to stop them from shaking. "It was after Blake smashed the rock over Cara's head that he ran back to the bonfire to get Jamie. He said he needed a little help." Garrett's face crinkles like a leaf as he repeats bitterly, "*A little help.*"

"So... she was already... "

He nods. "He took Jamie to the rocks and Jamie saw Cara lying there bleeding out her ear... and Blake told him she was dead, that she'd fallen. He lied to Jamie too."

A clock on the wall ticks off each second. Everyone else has left the waiting room to check on the ongoing commotion with Blake in the hallway, so the room is eerily silent... just me, Aunt Meg, Garrett, and his terrible story.

He looks at us, then his eyes wander blankly into space again. "Blake told Jamie that he owed it to him to fix this, to keep him from having to spend the rest of his life in prison. He 'owed' him, since Jamie got *his* girlfriend pregnant. Jamie... I dunno... I can't imagine how confused and devastated he must have been. He finds out all at the same time that Cara is pregnant, and now she's dead, and his best friend killed her, and..."

He runs his fingers through his hair. "So he panicked. He did what Blake told him to do. He got his jet ski, and they squeezed Cara between the two of them, and they drove the jet ski into the ocean, and..."

I squeeze my eyes shut.

"I just found this out," Garrett repeats, holding our gaze again as if desperate to convince us. "Just a few weeks ago... right before school started. When Jamie told me what had happened—at least what Blake *said* had happened, that it was an 'accident' like Blake insisted—I told Blake I'd keep his goddamn secret, mostly for Mom and Dad's sake, but I'd never let him out of my sight again. I told him I'd watch him like a hawk, that he better never slip up again..."

The irony settles over us like a damp, heavy blanket. "He would have killed him," Garrett adds in barely a whisper. "If we hadn't gone into the room at that exact moment, that bastard would have killed again. And maybe I'd be next. I'm the one who knew it wasn't an accident."

The words hang in the air, then he repeats them:

"He would have killed again."

EPILOGUE

"All the comforts of home."

Aunt Meg surveys my tiny dorm room, complete with cinderblock walls, and crosses her arms. "It'll look like home when I'm done with it," she assures me.

And I believe her. With her knickknacks and area rugs and curtains, she'll have this drab box looking fabulous within an hour. That's Aunt Meg.

She hugs me spontaneously. "This is gonna be so great."

I laugh at her earnestness, touched that she's so fiercely intent on making my world as warm and cozy as it can be.

Uncle Mark walks in behind us carrying the largest pieces of my luggage. A mini-refrigerator, laptop, area rug, and television set will be the last things to unload.

"I accept tips," he says, setting the luggage on the floor, and I offer him a fist bump.

My roommate, a fellow premed student named Layla from the West Coast, has texted me that her plane lands in an hour. Assuming she's not totally wiped out from the flight, she plans to grab a bite with Sawbones and me tonight for dinner. She and I have exchanged a few texts, photos, and emails, but otherwise I know nothing about her.

Suits me. Where's the challenge in living with someone you've actually met? I figure the odds that we'll be best friends a few weeks from now are approximately the same as us loathing each other. Well-meaning relatives and acquaintances have inundated me with their own freshman roommate stories lately, and none of them have any gray area. Apparently, randomly matched roommates are destined to be either soul mates or mortal enemies. Nobody ever seems to say, "My roommate was a nice-enough person," or, "Frankly, I was pretty indifferent about her." I've been warned to expect high drama on the roommate front, for better or worse. The good news is that Sawbones is in the next dorm over. As always, he'll be my touchstone when my life veers into Crazytown. Maybe I can even return the favor now and then. How cool would *that* be?

I smile at the thought as I pull a lamp out of a box. High drama? Craziness? Bring it on. I'm getting to be somewhat of a pro at it, if I do say so myself.

"Whatcha smiling about?" Aunt Meg asks as she places a stack of neatly folded T-shirts in a dresser drawer.

"Just … psyched about a fresh start," I say, and my spine actually tingles.

She pauses to smile back at me. "Me too."

Aunt Meg and I have gotten really close over the past

year. Yes, her perkiness still makes me wince (particularly when it goes into overdrive first thing in the morning), but she and Uncle Mark have been right by my side during my unwitting bit-part performance in the biggest scandal in Hollis Island history. Blake's trial is still pending, and the fact that Cara's body has never been recovered, coupled with the charm he's pouring on with a ladle on the local media, has some people suspecting he'll never spend a day behind bars.

But with Jamie and Garrett's testimony, who knows? Maybe justice will prevail for poor Cara. Jamie will probably get a pretty light sentence based on his cooperation with the prosecutors, but everybody who knows him agrees that he'll spend a lifetime imprisoning himself with guilt and self-loathing.

I really hope not. Yes, I want both Blake and Jamie held accountable for what they did that night, but I can't help having a soft spot for the quiet, tortured guy who paid the ultimate price for his allegiance to Blake. Christ, he almost paid with his *life*. That'll be a different trial, and one I'll no doubt get dragged into. But I can handle it. Garrett and I have stayed pretty tight since the whole debacle blew up in our faces, and we've resolved to have each other's backs. I've asked him more than once how he can manage living under the same roof with Blake as his brother's trial wends its way through the court system, and he says it's actually easier living with him now than it was before the truth came out.

That was the hardest thing he's ever done, Garrett says: keeping his brother's secret for those two weeks, thinking it was somehow in everybody's best interest, or at least *most* people's best interest. Garrett says his mother still vehemently defends Blake and won't stand for anybody speaking ill of him, so he and his dad simply humor her.

My friendship with Lauren survived the trauma—she's going to college closer to home than I am, and we'll stay in touch and see each other on holidays and occasional weekends. But although Mel and I are always totally friendly, our relationship was one of the casualties of Cara's murder. She never quite got over seeing Jamie's near-lifeless body in the bed that day, and she never would have started dating him if I hadn't started dating Blake. She's never said that explicitly, but the tentacles of the whole ugly mess just reach too far to give our friendship any breathing room. We never managed more than pleasant smiles and banal conversation for the rest of our senior year. She's going to college out west. I have a feeling I've seen and heard the last of her, but I wish her the best and am really happy she's getting a fresh start too.

I continued seeing Dr. Sennett through my whole senior year (you were prescient, Aunt Meg!), and she really helped me through some shaky times. It was hell learning to trust myself again after letting myself be lured into Blake's web of lies, but Dr. Sennett pointed out that I hadn't been fooled for long. I know it has a bit of a new-age vibe, but she's even posited the idea that maybe I was meant to cross Blake's path at that exact time to ensure justice for Cara and save Jamie's life. How's that for a noble spin?

I'll take it. I like the thought of destiny and grand schemes and big pictures. I'd never given much thought to an afterlife before Mom and Dad died, but I truly do feel connected to them in a very real way. Maybe some kind of cosmic string-pulling is going on. Or maybe I just like thinking so. Either way is fine. Either way, I'm gonna be okay.

I open a text from Sawbones: "*How's your view, E?*"

I glance out my dorm window to check it out and reply, "*It's a dumpster. Yours?*"

He writes back, "*My dorm's oceanfront.*"

I smile. Smartass.

"*Don't forget dinner tonight,*" he texts, and I respond, "*The Plaza, right?*"

"*Right, otherwise known as Rock-Bottom Burger Barrel on Fuller Street. Wear your leopard-print leggings, why don't you? See you at 6.*"

I snicker. "*Don't forget I'm bringing my roomie, assuming she doesn't flee in horror when she takes a gander at Aunt Meg's pink dotted-Swiss curtains.*"

Aunt Meg looks over at me as she hangs clothes in my closet and asks, "Who ya texting?"

"Sawbones," I say. "Hey, do you and Uncle Mark want to stay for dinner? Sawyer's meeting my roommate and me for burgers."

"Oooohhh, that sounds so collegiate!" Aunt Meg coos. "Count us in!"

"Done."

It'll be my little secret how relieved I am to have them by my side for a few more hours.

I pull out the next item from the box I'm unloading, and I smile at a picture of me with Mom and Dad. We're at one of Dad's company softball games, and we're all wearing ball caps and team shirts. The sun is in our eyes but we're beaming into the camera, our hair matted and our cheeks rosy with perspiration. I remember what a great day that was. I wipe the frame with a dust rag and place it on top of my dresser. Uncle Mark notices and gives me a wink.

I feel for a second that tears might spring into my eyes, but the moment passes. I'm still smiling, still excited, still optimistic about the first day of the rest of my life.

I press Mom and Dad's rings against my chest and reach for the next item in my box.

Acknowledgments

A huge thanks to my first and best readers/editors: Julianne Deriso, Taylor Deriso, Greg Deriso, and John Jenkins —amazing wordsmiths one and all, each with different strengths that enhanced my manuscript in myriad ways. I also thank the family and friends who endured my in-depth plot descriptions throughout the writing process, offering astute observations and great suggestions even when they had one ear peeled for the next question at our trivia games or needed to ring off the phone to get on with their, you know, lives. I offer my deepest appreciation to Ann Beth Strelec for jumpstarting this novel. Voluminous thanks also to Sara Crowe and Brian Farrey-Latz—agent and editor extraordinaire, respectively, along with the other stellar and encouraging staff at Harvey Klinger and Flux. Finally, my boundless gratitude to the bookends who have filled every moment of my life with love and inspiration: my parents, Gregory and Jane Hurley, and Dane Gregory Deriso, my goodest boy.

Nicole Renee Photography

About the Author

Christine Hurley Deriso is an award-winning author of the young adult novels *Then I Met My Sister* and *Thirty Sunsets*, along with four middle grade novels. She blogs weekly at goodreads.com. For ongoing updates, like her Christine Hurley Deriso author page on Facebook.